Short Stories – Autumn 2024

Back Roads Literary Review

Michael Van Natta, Editor

ISBN: 979-8-9916653-0-8 (Paperback) and 797-8-9916653-1-5 (EBOOK). Any references to historical events, real people, or real places are used fictitiously. Some of the places depicted are fictitious embellishments of actual places but beyond that, names, characters, and places are products of the author's imagination.

Copies of this book may be found at the Back Roads Literary Review website: backroadsliteraryreview.com

First printing edition 2024. Printed in USA.

Back Roads Literary Review
1699 Highway 14
Knoxville, IA 50138
www.backroadsliteraryreview.com

Table of Contents

FOREWORD

Welcome, fans of scary stories! As Halloween approaches, we take time to gather up stories to tell around the campfire bundled up against the chill winds of Autumn. Trees have shed their leaves and summer has been laid to rest over the decaying ground. At a time when the year's harvest is over and preparation for the long dark months of winter has yet to begin, it is a time for wool-gathering, both literally and figuratively.

This edition of the *Back Roads Literary Review* Scary Story Anthology brings together stories of the paranormal and the supernatural. The Anthology has its roots in just such late-season campfires – twenty annual gatherings of writers from our workshop with scary original fiction in hand and delivered aloud between hamburgers and s'mores under dark night skies and glowing pumpkin eyes.

Within these pages, we present Stephen Brayton's story of paranormal investigators driven to a haunting and bitter end, entitled *Dead House*. Kendall Klym gives us a tale of spirits haunting Church establishments and subtle secrets buried deep with the text of *The Incorruptible Corpse*, a tale that spans centuries. In *Echoes of Revenge*, Deb Miller spins a tale of an archeologist who must learn to control her strange psychometric abilities that allow a deeper empathy with the dead. *Gold Fever* by Joann Schissel, set in the wild west of the 1800's, follows a thief coming to his just reward. Cats, especially black ones, invoke the spirit of the season and have reputations for bringing bad luck. But that's just an old wives' tale, isn't it? Decide for yourself by immersing in *Speaking the Language*. Have you ever been trapped in an elevator? Caught in an endlessly revolving door? Ever run out of gas, wishing you'd just stopped at that last service station – the one with the sign that said Next Gas 62 miles in bold black hand-painted letters? In *Middle Ground*, the protagonist and all around confused dude named Hal demonstrates that good characters – are well, mostly good.

Michael Van Natta
Editor in Chief

Dead House

Stephen L. Brayton

"Watch out!" Drake yelled.

An extended horn blast from the semi filled the interior of the van. Drake lunged for the steering wheel, but Taryn jerked the wheel right. The van swerved back into the proper lane. The semi, driver still blaring the horn, rushed past, missing the van by mere inches.

Drake squeezed shut his eyes, felt the buffeting air push against the side of the vehicle. For a second, he imagined he heard the momentary crunch of steel against steel, the irresistible object—the extended cab—smashing against the smaller equipment van. His heart stopped for a moment, the adrenaline and terror-induced thumping went silent.

When he opened his eyes, he expected to see darkness, nothingness, but breathed in relief when Highway 4 stretched north. The sun had moved behind a bank of clouds. Very little of the blue sky showed above.

Taryn stepped on the brake and eased the van onto the gravel shoulder. Drake thought she was going to express shock and relief at his last second warning that she'd drifted over the center line in the midst of arguing with him. Instead, she verbally lashed out. "You almost got us killed."

"You're driving," Drake countered. "Pay attention to the damn road."

"Shut the hell up, and I will," Taryn said. She must have

lifted her foot from the brake because the van, still in Drive, crept forward. Taryn stomped on the brake, the van came to a stop with the minutest of skids, and she yanked the gear to Park. Then she folded her arms across the wheel and rested her forehead on the top wrist.

"Don't do this, Drake," she said. "Not today."

"I'm not 'doing' anything," he said. "It's not like I made the decision in the last five minutes. This has been on my mind for a few weeks."

She raised her head and sat back in the seat. "Well, you picked a helluva time to tell me, you know, on the way to the next investigation. If you wanted to quit, why didn't you say something earlier when we discussed this trip?"

"Because I was halfway interested in this particular haunted house. That doesn't change the fact that I've been thinking about ... well, you know."

"Quitting," she said.

Drake inhaled and released a deep breath. "I'm getting tired, Taryn. After seven years of these paranormal investigations, I'm fed up. With the long travel times. Of staying in cheap motels and eating diner food or worse. Tired of too many of these places being so fake you can spot the special effects as we roll up the driveway."

"Not all of them are like that," Taryn said.

"Enough that we lose money on them. Not like we're making any sort of profit anyway."

"We didn't get into this to become rich."

Drake took another deep breath and shook his head in resignation. "Look, we're talking in circles. We've been over this for the last fifteen minutes."

"Yeah, and look where it's gotten us. On the shoulder of the straightest damn state highway, in the middle of freakin' Iowa after almost getting creamed by a semi that came outta nowhere." Taryn pointed out the windshield. "Look, you can see for three miles. Where the hell did it come from?"

"I wasn't paying attention," Drake said. "Neither were you."

"All right, shut up already."

Taryn jerked the gear back to Drive, glanced out the side mirror, and pulled back onto the highway.

Drake opted for staring out his window at the passing corn and bean fields, most of them harvested, this being late October. Some of the fields showed the rounded rows of overturned earth, all ready for winter to strip away the nutrient-filled topsoil. Most were left with broken stalks of corn or brown, weedy remains of the bean crop to endure the upcoming months, the farmers electing to wait until the spring to plow.

Farm houses of white-painted wood or red brick backed by silos of various heights dotted the landscape. Gravel country roads intersected Highway 4 every quarter or half mile.

Drake wished he was back in Peoria, where he and Taryn lived. They'd met in high school and became friends mainly due to their mutual interest in the paranormal and supernatural. Ghosts, haunted buildings, monster myths, and urban legends that told of lonely highways, dark woods, old cemeteries (of course), and a variety of venues and locales. They were fans of any paranormal investigation television show.

After college, they both found decent-paying jobs but spent many weekends and vacations traveling to conduct their own research, using saved money to buy a van, food, motel stays, and the equipment they needed.

Mildly successful at first, they discovered "happenings" that they couldn't explain. They ran into many more fakes and hoaxes and easily revealed "hauntings." After seven years, Drake was tired of it all. Too many weekends on the road. Hell, he didn't have time to go out, date anyone, or develop a steady romantic relationship. He and Taryn once flirted with the idea of being a couple, spent one weekend together doing things not ghost-related, but afterward decided that while they enjoyed each other's company, romance didn't fit into the scenario.

Drake hadn't exactly lied when he said he agreed to go on this current trip. He was interested but had expressed dubiousness and skepticism about the veracity of the reports. His agreement came after Taryn all but badgered him into it, and he swore this was the last trip. He felt the need to live a "normal" life, find a wife, have a few kids, and climb up the corporate ladder at least three or four more rungs.

He'd brought up the subject of his ... yes, quitting the team, earlier, which spurred on the argument.

A sharp sting against his outer thigh from a swift backhand slap from Taryn.

"Hey, why don't you review for us what we're getting into," she said. "Maybe rereading the material will get you out of your funk."

Not likely, he thought, but it was her way of moving past the heated discussion and persuade him to get his mind back to why they were on the road.

He reached behind his seat to the leather briefcase/laptop carrier and set it on his lap. Remembering which pouch contained the paperwork, he withdrew the folder. From it, he removed a clipped stack of papers and read from the first sheet.

"The house was built in the mid 1860's when Iowa was still a relatively young state. Franklin MacLaren and his family chose the location because it offered protective woodland and rich farmland. Plus, it was only a day's journey to the growing town of Emmetsburg."

"Which didn't burgeon into a major city," Taryn said.

"True, but it was the closest settlement for supplies. It incorporated in 1877."

"Didn't I read the house is technically part of a conservation area?"

"The Watson Heritage Area, but that came later. And way later than the MacLarens who didn't last three years." Drake pursed his lips and skimmed the subsequent paragraphs. "They were the first victims of ... whatever was wrong with the location or the house."

"Yeah, pretty weird," Taryn said. "A neighbor—'neighbor' being relative since he lived three miles away—stopped by and found the entire family—Franklin, his wife, and four children—dead. Lying all over the house and front lawn. No obvious cause of death. No blood. No signs of violence. Nothing. Just dead, like they all suffered simultaneous heart attacks."

"That's not the only weird part. They were seen on their way back from Emmetsburg shortly before the neighbor stopped for a visit."

"Read me that part again," Taryn said.

Drake felt the change in the van's sped as if Taryn unconsciously slowed, lengthening the trip to hear the story.

"Another neighbor heading into town said he came upon the MacLaren's wagon overturned off the road. The family stood nearby, apparently uninjured. The guy helped right the wagon and that was that."

"But that wasn't that," Taryn said.

"Correct. Later, after the family was found dead, the man who helped them reported the MacLarens didn't say anything, not even a token thank you. They all stared at him, which he considered a somewhat acknowledgment of his assistance, then rode off."

"Who was next?" Taryn asked.

"You really get into these things," Drake said.

"Like stories around a campfire."

Drake found the next section. "The house sat empty for about six months before the Dergans moved in."

"They weren't there a full year," Taryn said.

"If you know all this, why am I reading it?"

"Just to have it fresh in my mind when we get there," she said.

"Yep, ten months later, the same neighbor who discovered the MacLarens visited to find the Dergans dead. Again, on the floor in the house or outside on the ground. Being winter, one theory was they froze, but that was dismissed when they realized the body in the house lay next to the wood stove that was down to coals, but had to have been aflame for at least an hour. The marshall questioned the neighbor, suspecting foul play, but nothing came of it."

"And the other weird similarity to the MacLarens?"

"Well, the Dergans were childless, so no similarity there," Drake said. "However, while in Emmetsburg, Larry Dergan and his wife narrowly avoided injury or worse when a couple of spooked horses broke free of their owner's reins." He turned the page. "After that, a few more families moved in over the next ten years despite the reputation of the house. None lived more than two years and every family ended up dead under the same mysterious circumstances."

"And those deaths happened after each family experienced an accident."

Drake reread the reports even though he'd looked over them the previous day. "The day of or the day before their deaths or discovery of the bodies. One family helping at a nearby farm barely escaped a barn fire. Another overturned wagon in the middle of a blizzard. A single man survived a gunshot wound from a fleeing robber in Emmetsburg."

"And no one has lived there since," Taryn said.

Drake nodded. "Place sat empty, probably to fall into ruin by now."

"Did you not read the rest?"

Drake sighed. "Skimmed it. You know, I was debating with myself on whether to go on this trip, so I stopped after the last death."

"Reports over the years from various sources say that the place has aged, but didn't deteriorate like you'd expect. People who've seen it, not up close, say it looks pretty much intact"

Drake shrugged.

"There have been a handful of paranormal investigations done on it and a couple of people have wound up dead there, too. How do you explain all those deaths?" Taryn asked.

"Mold? A fast-acting virus? Arsenic in the wood? A contaminant in the water or food that built up over time."

"But all family members dropped dead at the same time. And those investigators hadn't been there too long. There wouldn't have been enough time for something in the water to build up in their systems."

"You have a theory?" Drake asked. "Simultaneous heart attacks or aneurysms?"

"I don't know?"

"Bad juju on former Indian land? An unknown curse from some chief who got booted out of his home?"

"Maybe."

"Invisible monster from the woods who sucked out the life spirits?"

"Now, you're being silly," Taryn said.

"No, remember that place in Kentucky we visited? The locals talked of a creature like that."

"The locals were trying to put one over on us," Taryn said. "Most of them had consumed way too much of their homemade moonshine."

"True, but it was a decades' old legend in that area." Drake smiled and returned to the theories of their current case. "Silly would have been aliens beaming down a death ray."

"Right," Taryn said. "But what about the accidents right before all these people died?"

Drake shrugged. "Could be coincidence?"

"You believe that?"

Drake didn't know what to believe or think. Actually, he didn't care. His enthusiasm for this case ran low.

"I don't know," he repeated. "I guess we'll do our best to find out."

Taryn apparently wouldn't let him go into a good brood. "When did this place acquire its nickname?"

Drake studied the pages. "Locals started calling it Dead House right before the last death."

"Read me that part."

Even though Drake knew she already knew, he decided to play along. What the hell, one more investigation wasn't going to hurt. He might as well act a little interested. "Various sightings of ghosts and the usual mysterious lights and sounds throughout the decades," he said. "Eventually, it fell into a 'local legend' category. It didn't become a tourist attraction like that house in ... what's that town over in western Iowa? Barista?"

"Villisca, you jerk."

"Just kidding."

"That one was fun," she said."

"Right," Drake said. "You say you saw one of the ghosts."

"I did."

"Yet everyone around you saw nothing."

Taryn's turn to shrug. "What can I say. Maybe some of the spirits like me better. Anyway, get back to Dead House."

"As you said a few ghost hunters and the like have visited. And there have been at least a half dozen more deaths over the decades."

"Pretty spooky, no?"

No, he thought. "Maybe. What's this article?" He read

about the most recent death of a ghost hunter. "'Last seen near Emmetsburg. Mother received final phone call from son who said he was on State Highway 4.'"

"Same as we are," Taryn said.

"'Police investigated legendary Dead House. Body found. No clues to cause of death.'"

"And no other investigative teams found anything," Taryn said.

Drake gave her a look that said, Yet we've traveled over six hours.

He caught Taryn's glance before she turned back to the road. Drake checked the GPS on the phone she'd stuck to a dash magnet. It showed they were about three miles south of Emmetsburg. Looking out the windshield, he saw the small sign with a green background and white letters and numbers indicating they were at—now past—420th Street.

This part of Iowa, he thought, resembled the majority of the state. Yes, he understood Iowa was not flat, but this road consisted of gradual hills.

Again, he gazed out the passenger window. How he wished he was home to meet up with some friends, accept the ever-present invitation for a round of golf. He and Taryn probably would spend the night either at Dead House or at a motel in Emmetsburg. Which meant no chance to hit any Peoria nightclubs.

Drake inwardly groaned. Making sleeping arrangements in a supposedly haunted house, a spooky cave or an abandoned hospital was exciting in the beginning. Even left with no other feasible option than to spend the night in tents added to the thrill.

He now remembered those sleepless nights. Not because of ghosts or things that went bump in the night, but because of the hard and uneven ground, indigestion and heartburn from bad food, animal noises—damned owls hooting all night—weather, or sleeping in an unfamiliar location, especially when they stayed in regular lodging.

And what were the results of those years of traveling? Nationally recognized for proving the existence of ghosts and creepies? Interviews on morning talk shows? Best-selling books? Invited to join any television paranormal hunting team?

No to all of those questions. No recognition, no interviews, books, or guest appearances. Instead, they spent thousands of dollars on second-hand equipment that glitched as often as it functioned properly, a van that eked out fifteen miles per gallon on a good day, second-rate motels, and cheap food.

For what? Discovering rats in the walls, kids pranking the locals, natural phenomena such as marsh gas and phosphorescent plants and animals, none of it eerie or scary.

Okay, there were a few places that were ... inexplicable. The overwhelming sense of dread felt by both Taryn and him as well as a short-lived trance Taryn experienced at the Bellaire House in Ohio. Footsteps and laughter from an invisible entity in a New Jersey parking garage. One of the weirdest incidents occurred in a haunted junkyard. Well, it wasn't a junkyard, per se, but a collection of old, rusted-out vans, cars, buses, and delivery trucks arranged in two circles in the woods south of Knoxville, Iowa. Taryn and Drake spent the night just off the outer circle and heard nothing. However, in the morning, a dozen vehicles had switched locations.

Still, the majority of their investigations were dull and boring. Drake suspected that this trip to Dead House would be the next in a long line of duds. If he had his way, it would be the last in line. He hoped he could convince Taryn that he was serious about quitting, especially when she popped by his apartment with a folder containing material for the next ghostly adventure.

His attention shifted out the windshield. Thick woodland appeared to the northwest. Yellow painted letters carved into a wooden sign read Watson Heritage Area with an arrow pointing west. Taryn slowed and turned left onto a gravel road, 400th Street. Almost a mile later, they passed a rutted road that Drake figured was for maintenance vehicles.

"There should be another dirt road that will lead us to Dead House," Taryn said. "Before we left, I looked at Google Maps, but it didn't show up."

Another mile passed, and they neared a bridge that looked like it was built by the low-bid contractor. Two rusty steel rail barriers to deter vehicles driving off but nothing on either side of the gravel road to prevent driving into the creek. And it wasn't a true creek, more like a trough. Ditch #21 read the simple sign.

Thirty yards before the bridge a wide spot evidenced a rarely-used rutted and deteriorated road into the trees. Actually, road was an overstatement. Path was more apt.

Taryn slowed. Drake craned his head forward to have a better look. The path all but petered out ten yards into the trees. Nature was well on its way to reclaiming the former "driveway" with underbrush, tall grass, and a scattering of saplings.

"I think this is it," Taryn said.

"You think," Drake said, skepticism coating his words.

"It has to be."

Taryn eased the van off the gravel, across a fifty-foot section of grass, and jounced onto the dirt path. Drake grabbed the handle attached to the roof above the door and leaned forward to try to see the way through the trees. Taryn maneuvered the van past trunks that missed the side mirrors by inches. Brown, weedy underbrush scour-padded the undercarriage. Only faint tracks and breadcrumbs of beer cans, plastic baggies, and even a ripped T-shirt showed the way. This far north in Iowa, most of the leaves carpeted the ground, but the area still boasted species of firs that shielded the view in places.

The van jolted when the left front tire dropped into a deep rut. The undercarriage scraped the ground like the edge of a trowel run over a brick. Drake's grip on the handle prevented him from a face-plant on the dash. Recovering, he saw Taryn's tightened grip on the wheel and set jaw as she increased acceleration enough to roll the tire up the far side of the depression. Drake waited and prepared for the rear tire. The back end tilted, and the bumper brushed the ground.

Then they were on level ground. The path wound off to the northeast out of sight of the main road. Gradually, it angled back toward the water trough of Ditch #21. Drake judged a bit more than a quarter mile before the path acquired more definition and widened as it approached a clearing. Taryn braked at the perimeter.

The house stood in the general center of the clearing which measured at least seventy yards in diameter. While early settlers built their homes from sod because of the scarcity of the wood, the MacLarens were fortunate no others had built in the area before they arrived. They had cleared this large section of woodland and used a portion of the timber for the house. Drake wondered where Franklin did his farming. Perhaps there had been a field at some point, but after the place had been abandoned, the trees grew back.

The house itself was aged but the wood not rotted. Holes and warping, but generally intact, even livable if given some care and patches in strategic places. One story, but larger than many of the simple, early homes of the prairie. Perhaps Franklin had extra time and resources or he expected a lengthy stay with more planned offspring.

A dilapidated outbuilding, an early barn or storage shed, lay off the house's rear right flank. It looked ready for grain or perhaps a few cows or horses.

The condition of the house competed for attention with the clearing. While the residence wasn't brand new, it lay on the opposite side of the spectrum from what surrounded it. Dead, brown grass, bare in many patches. Ten yards out from the clearing, the ring of trees stood leafless and lifeless far beyond the fall dormancy. Knotty branches and twisted trunks evidenced a strange and unnatural growth pattern.

"Whoa!" Taryn uttered on a breathy voice.

Drake agreed but not for the same reason. He thought his partner in the paranormal had a frisson of excitement, and anticipation surging through her. Drake had one of ... finality. Not dread. Not fear. Somehow, he understood on an instinctual level, even if he couldn't verbally express it that they'd reached the goal of every paranormal investigative team. To find actual evidence of the supernatural however one defined it. This place was that evidence.

Taryn eased the van forward. Drake wanted to tell her, to plead with her, to yell at her to reverse, to forget this whole trip, to go home.

Too late. They entered the clearing, and Drake went numb. Regret bore down on him. Regret for accepting this trip. Regret for not doing more with his life than spending years on these silly ghost chases. Regret for ... everything.

It was a strange emotion to have, and he couldn't shake it away. The worst regret was the knowledge, again, fathomed from deep inside him, that he couldn't make up for not going down another path with his life.

His breaths came labored and heavy, like trying to get oxygen out of a dense, tangible, but invisible fog.

"Are you okay?" Taryn asked.

Drake quivered a nod but, that was a lie. Taryn must have misinterpreted his behavior as silent thrill of seeing everything and wanting to know more.

"Let's explore before we set up the equipment," she said. "Hell, we might be able to spend the night in the house instead of the tents."

Taryn pushed open her door, hopped out, and practically ran to the house's front entrance. Drake saw strips of leather nailed to the timber to act as hinges. Taryn put the tips of her fingers on the flat of the door and ran them down to a notch which she pulled on to open the door. She didn't enter and didn't look back at him. Instead, she stared at the interior.

Drake popped open his door and slid out of the van. He walked to where Taryn, still not moving, stood at the house's threshold. From over her shoulder, he looked inside. Where he expected to find broken furniture, dusty cupboards and cabinets, maybe a desk, table, or even beds, there was ... nothing. Just darkness.

However, there was enough sunlight coming in to see a group of people in the front room. Men, women, and children in period clothing from the late 1800s through the 1970s. All standing, looking at Taryn and him. Not moving, not blinking, not speaking. Blank expressions, but Drake sensed sadness ... regret.

In an instant, Drake understood the sensation that had befallen him when they entered the clearing. These were the previous inhabitants and visitors to the house. Families, couples, the lone bachelor, and the investigators who didn't return. How many in all? Twenty, give or take.

Drake remembered the material he had skimmed before Taryn and he started on the trip and then had reread not twenty minutes before. All the notes and the history of the place. More specifically, how the place had earned its nickname. The deaths. And not just the simultaneous deaths, but the surrounding circumstances. What came before others people found their bodies.

Accidents. Overturned wagons. A gunshot. A fire. Soon after, the victims of these near-deaths had died.

No, Drake thought, and turned to find the proof of the truth that had hit him when he saw the people in the house.

He looked at the van Taryn and he had used to come to Iowa. The front end crumpled, headlights smashed, grill twisted. Windshield and windows shattered. Two tires flat.

As if a monstrous semi had crashed into the vehicle head on.

One had, and Taryn and he hadn't survived. They had continued their trip ... just like everyone else who hadn't survived their "accidents." They had finished their journeys, reached their destination, and never left.

Drake tuned back to Taryn who looked at him. Her expression showed him she'd deduced everything before he had.

She kept his gaze for a long moment, then faced the people standing in the room. Another moment passed before she stepped across the threshold.

Drake took one last look at the empty, deceased clearing and the destroyed van. Then, he, too, stepped into the entry to join Taryn and the rest of the dead in Dead House.

The Incorruptible Corpse

Kendall Klym

Rome, 31 May 1578

After a rainstorm, a winegrower enters his vineyard. With a deeply lined and leathery hand, he checks the canes, cordons, and canopy. He crosses himself. With God presiding, he knows the ripening grapes will blossom into the Blood of Christ. As the grower moves down the row, a peculiar sensation—not unlike a puff of fresh air—tickles his loins. Like Jesus, he turns his head from the sun. Adjusting his tunic, he kneels, walks on his knees toward the source of the breeze. Near the downed branches of an ancient oak, he enters a hollow. At its center, he discovers a crevice in the fine tufa soil. Something is down there: that he knows.

Vineyard workers wield their mattocks and spades through ejectimenta from Rome's Pleistocenian volcanoes. By the end of the day, everyone is asking: What lies at the bottom? Something sinister or sacred? Two days later, workers unearth human remains. Skeletons—many intact and very old.

The Roman Catholic elite devise a plan: use the remains to strike back at Protestant reformers with evidence—the bodies of Saints—proof that Catholicism reigns supreme. But what makes the Papists think God Almighty picked these scraggly skeletons for veneration? The answer is easy. The excavators have rediscovered the Roman Catacombs. The people who had filled these venerable bones died in the Early Christian Era.

Because they had sacrificed their lives for their faith, they were martyrs and qualify categorically as Saints.

So what to do? Turn over the remains to the Vatican for examination and certification. Summon couturiers to dress up the Saints as opulently as possible. Instruct couriers to carry the Saints across the Alps to German-speaking lands—places where Protestants have wreaked the most damage. Convince Catholics and Protestants alike of God's rewards for those who follow unwaveringly the Catholic faith. Revel in the outcome: bones hidden beneath wormlike strands of filigree wire encrusted with warty pearls. Rubies and emeralds filling in for flesh, like pustules of petrified blood and scabs ravaged by gangrene. Martyrdom at its best.

Midvale Monastery, Nebraska, May 31, 2024
An overnight deluge inundates the wine cellar at Midvale Monastery, located in a dale flanked by the Gower River. A few feet from rows of bottles of sweet Nebraska Riesling, the concrete floor erodes and breaks away. Decomposing and lying in the muddy water are a couple of caskets. After tending the vineyard, two monks enter the wine cellar. They lower themselves into the murk and open the caskets. Inside the first is a skeleton, undoubtedly male. The second features another male, except this one's failed to decompose. Skin leathery and orange-gray, the corpse wears a monk's habit—faded and covered with mold but still intact.

Tests are completed. Word spreads fast, and pilgrims come to see the body of an unknown monk, estimated to have died in the second decade of the twentieth century. Bishop Patrick O'Lanolin of the Platte-Watervliet Diocese warns pilgrims not to touch or venerate the body of the dead monk. Unofficial reports claim the body may be incorruptible—a Catholic term referring to human remains that have resisted decomposition after death. Yet the classification of incorruptible fails to ensure the status of sainthood, according to the Church. Pilgrims refuse to heed the bishop's warning. Reporters and talk-show hosts inundate the rural monastery, known for its peaceful setting far from any highway or city.

The corpse is moved to the church and placed under glass beneath the altar. On the grounds of the monastery, a 33-year-old seminarian completing a Master of Arts in Catholic Studies two states away, gets run over by an SUV. The culprit is a middle-aged fashion designer driving while texting pictures of the dead monk to friends in New York. Though the seminarian survives the accident, he will lose his legs according to doctors.

Nebraska Hospital, June 1, 2024
Nobody takes notice when I enter at 3 in the morning. The Brothers have been coming and going for half the night. My hood hangs low, so I don't scare anyone. I look straight ahead as I head for the seminarian's room. The man's asleep. His expression—mouth slightly open, lips curved upward in a peaceful smile—reminds me of the monk I fell in love with. It was a hundred years ago today, when the Abbot discovered my letters, when Jonathan and I dug a deep hole in the wine cellar, buried ourselves, and died soon after, lying in each other's arms. When a Brother discovered us a few days later, the Abbot put us in caskets, sealed up the hole, and made the Brothers swear to eternal secrecy. Jonathan moved on, while I wallowed in guilt. If only I had I refrained from writing, from taking the first step, from professing my love. That's how I used to think. A hundred years is a long time to spend as a recovering Catholic. Long enough. It's time for me to move on. I take off my legs and do some measurements and adjustments. Good thing the seminarian has a body similar to mine.

Midvale Monastery and Nebraska Hospital, June 1-2, 2024

The abbot discovers the missing corpse and drinks a bottle of Riesling. A Type 2 diabetic, he's rushed to the hospital and kept overnight. The next morning, the seminarian gets out of bed and walks downstairs to visit the abbot. Both amputations are canceled. After dark, a legless corpse, hands dirtier and body drenched in sweat, reappears at the monastery. Reporters rush back to Nebraska. Pilgrims follow. They purchase and drink lots of wine. Bishop O'Lanolin refrains from telling them not to venerate the legless corpse. The bishop reads to the monks from the *Rule of St. Benedict*: "Brothers, Divine Scripture calls to us saying: 'Whoever exalts himself shall be humbled, and whoever humbles himself shall be exalted.' " Known for his denouncement of homosexuality, the bishop announces plans to begin the process of canonization of the incorruptible corpse.

Speaking the Language

Michael Van Natta and Joann Schissel

Some people throw out junk as soon as it weighs too much. Others never get around to clearing out the crap gathered year after year by the very act of living. And some hoard it. Relish it. Feed on it.

I moved to our acreage we affectionately named Cozy Corner with my husband, Luke, two years ago. Seven acres in the rolling country hills on the highway four miles from the town of Harmony. Cozy Corner was a dream come true.

Luke was only thirty-eight and you'd have thought that he'd be sapped of energy. He wasn't. He'd often say to me, "Francie, I'm going to make everything perfect for you." What was left unspoken was how little time we had left together.

We got the place cheap, what with the scrap yard adjacent. I convinced him that the scud of trees lining the fence between our properties obscured most of the menagerie of assorted trashed cars, rusted oil drums, and a bulldozer.

Mr. Antree, owner of the junkyard, had to be somewhere in his late sixties. We first met him one evening at the town's Board of Supervisors meeting to discuss our property zoning. He wore grubby denim overalls that stretched over his hulking frame. Deep wrinkles around his narrow eyes and the down-turned corners of his mouth gave him a leering look.

At the meeting, we were surprised to learn our growly neighbor had a vested interest in a portion of our acreage. A shared easement running along the western edge of our grassy field provided the only way to drive into his property from the highway. With his access road along the fence line our property, he was allowed to voice any concerns about zoning.

Luke and I sat unbelieving as Antree demanded we install drainage tiles under the shared portion of the area that puddled up when it rained. Of course, all at our expense. He proffered his wishes with a halting cadence in a gruff voice, as if it had emanated from some cave. When his request was dismissed as absurd by Missy Percival, the zoning commissioner. I suspected we'd just made enemies with our new neighbor.

We refused to let the cantankerous collector stain our days and my enthusiastic husband got busy. He graded the yard with a rented skid loader. Planted seed and grew a lush lawn. I learned to operate the riding mower and banish weeds. The old farmhouse got a new coat of paint inside and out. We'd never been so close and happy in our shared commitment.

That first fall, he dug in bulbs and plopped in nursery plants. He lived to see the summer colors. Most people think of cancer as a withering depleting thief, a disfiguring monster. My man, though, put that notion to bed.

And to bed we went. The effort of hard toil, the sweat and sore muscles, the scourge that was his daily accomplice forgotten, he conjured up the vitality of youth, the desire of existence, and we pleasantly commingled along. He wanted more than anything to plant his seed in us. To forever carry on.

One summer day, before he passed, the evening sun had sunk low on the horizon, casting a pink glow across the backyard deck. With the remnants of dinner on our plates and wine glasses in hand, we lounged content over the majesty we'd brought to bear.

Appearing out of nowhere, a scrawny black cat strayed into our lives. Collarless and curious, she unabashedly begged for whatever scraps we could offer.

She especially took to Luke, who avowed at every turn how he was a dog person, disliking the aloof unspeaking nature of cats. He quickly succumbed to her charm.

In return for my husband's newly acquired feline tolerance and generosity, Tramp the cat flourished. We reveled in her presence, unaware of the gift she would soon present to us.

Tramp's tiny black kitten was delivered under our front porch. Somehow, our wise mama cat knew we'd take care of her and in return, we received a single, mewing clone. We named the squirming ball of black fur, Ditto.

Job complete, Tramp sickened later that fall. We found her body curled up under the same porch where Ditto was born.

Luke died a week later.

We grieved, Ditto and I, and following Luke's example, soldiered on without words. Suffering in our losses.

***

Ditto went from outdoor cat to indoor and learned the few rules of the household with ease. I, on the other hand, went through an arduous acquisition curve toward mastery of cat-speak. I worked on becoming fluent in one area only to be immediately confronted with another obscure sound or body language I didn't yet know. Ditto was a good, if frustrated teacher, rewarding me with snuggles and purring when I apparently got something right.

My constant companion was a quiet creature. But there's a reason the word "expression" defines both a figure of speech and the way one's face conveys an inner milieu. Ditto, it turned out, was skilled in the latter, capable of expressions that required the discernment of an artist or detective. But mostly, I learned her language by careful observation.

Mornings, she'd sneak through the crack of the bedroom door, hop up onto the bed and stand there with her determined face inches from mine until I awoke and climbed out from under the warm comforter to fill her food bowl.

Sometimes I had nightmares of being lost in a dark landscape searching for something. When I'd jolt awake from the fitful sleep, there she'd be. Tenacious, as if to say, "Get over it."

I'd watch mindless TV in the evenings, usually some Hallmark rom-com or incessant cable news to fill my emptiness. Ditto seemed to have a sense of what I needed to cheer me up. She'd leap up onto the couch and stare at me with her quizzical face. If I ignored her, she would begin her antics of circling and pouncing upon some invisible prey. I called it cat dancing. She'd continue her performance until she had my full attention. I'd chuckle and scratch her ears. Once noticed, she'd cozy up and sit on my lap. Ditto knew how to pull me away from my sadness. Her glistening eyes would convey a stare-me-down look, an insistence for me to keep going.

Poking me with her paw meant she wanted a chin rub. Circling her food bowl meant she needed me to feed her. Once I acquiesced, she'd snuggle up, having again been the successful teacher. And yes, I found her warm purring body a comfort, driving away notions of loneliness and self-pity.

***

As it happened, old Mr. Antree would make occasional appearances on the easement, driving back to the junkyard in his clattering old pickup, usually pulling a trailer loaded with a heap of rusted metal. Luke had concocted stories that Antree was a burglar, a bank-robber, or a safe-cracker, who laundered his ill-gotten cash in scrap metal. When I'd scoff, he'd tell me about the latest quote on the value of scrap steel. So, much as I reviled the old man, and much as I disliked the eyesore he kept, when he'd rattle through his gateway at the back corner of the property, it reminded me of Luke's crime stories. When his visits became more frequent and began to occur after midnight, the nostalgia of Luke's tales turned more toward concern.

It was about that time that I went into Harmony, to visit with Missy Percival.

"I get it, Francie," Missy said. "Yes, if you want, we can pursue this, but I doubt you'll get very far with it. His land is out of the city limits where we can't do much about it."

"It's just so ugly, Missy, all that crap. It smells bad, too, like oil and diesel fuel. Not only that, but he's also been using the easement late at night. I've seen headlights. The clanging noises from his truck wakes me up."

Missy shrugged her shoulders. "I'm sorry, Francie. He has a right to go to his property at night. Have you talked to the EPA about the junk? The petroleum leakage? I can give you a form to fill out." She shuffled some papers on her desk and picked up a newspaper.

"Did you hear about poor Belinda Coleman?"

I shook my head. "Who's that?"

Missy showed me the headlines of the *Harmony Gazette*.

ANOTHER GIRL MISSING

"Horrible, thing," Missy said. "What's happening to this town? We never had this kind of thing here before. The cops are going ape-shit and the mayor is apoplectic."

Walking across the street to the coffee shop with the multi-page EPA form, I remembered when we first moved to the property. There had been a story of a missing girl then, too. Never found. We were so busy, though, and I hadn't paid much attention.

At the coffee shop, a group of retired ladies huddled together at the corner table pouring over the *Gazette*. They prattled about the missing girl and conspired about who the likely suspect might be. I'd never been a part of that gossip scene, but I listened from a nearby table, drinking my coffee, while they speculated about their theories.

Harold's name came up. Everyone knew Harold, the unfortunate and dull-witted man who was the butt of all jokes and the cause of everything wrong in Harmony. He was also Antree's righthand man.

***

Ditto began to leave *gifts* placed purposely outside the back door, usually in the form of a small rodent. She insisted on maintaining an indoor-outdoor existence, so I didn't dare declaw her, but I did make sure she was spayed. All kinds of wildlife threats to her lurked beyond our doors. Stray tomcats, raccoons, a local fox, neighbor's dogs and birds of prey. I'd often see buzzards circling overhead and worried when she roamed outside.

She'd creep up with stealth on anything that moved. Didn't matter. Grasshoppers were especially fun for her because they jumped up as well as out. Kind of a 3-D game and Ditto loved to leap into the air. Birds, too, but not too often. Mice, of course, sometimes ground squirrels.

Whatever prey I'd been gifted, Ditto would stand guard with a look of the pride of accomplishment on her little face. If I didn't notice it and went about my chores, she'd take offense and like a herding collie, would circle me endlessly, "Come on, don't play games. Let's go look at what I brought you."

The motionless nature of her catch often fooled me into thinking it was dead. Ditto would display a face like someone telling a joke, knowing the punchline was coming. She'd sit nearby, nonchalant, as if to say, *Let's see what other mischief I can get into* face. She'd circle and walk a short distance away, deceiving the possum-playing animal until it lurched up and made a break for it. The games would start all over. And sometimes, if the prey was valiant enough, or Ditto just not hungry enough, she'd let it get away. I was torn by which to root for.

Sometimes, she'd want to go out so badly that she'd show me her sullen look and scratch on the wooden door frame until I opened the door. Out she'd go. I wouldn't see her until evening. Sometimes a day or two would go by without her coming home and I'd search for her, worried she got into some kind of trouble. I had seen her ambling into the junkyard, but I always hesitated to cross the boundary in my search. Something creepy about the place gave me chills.

On one occasion, she returned from a foray and stood by the door, refusing to come in when I opened it for her. She applied her determined face and paced back and forth, repeating this unusual behavior. When I tried to coerce her inside, she scurried just out of my reach and stop to look back at me. I grabbed my jacket and followed her toward the junkyard.

She led me to a pile of bones. Small cream-colored skulls, cleaned of all flesh and all brains, were scattered about in the dirt just over the fence in the junkyard. Femurs the size of pencils and shoulder blades the size of toy saucers were probably the remains of unfortunate small animals. The bones were in such a state of decay that they must have been around awhile. Maybe older than Ditto herself. I shuddered, puzzled about where they had come from. I swooped Ditto up in my arms and headed back to the house, hoping somehow, she'd learn to stay out of Antree's squalid domain. But cats have their own ideas.

***

The days became shorter and some of the trees had begun to

lose their leaves. That day the weather had been warmer than normal and late afternoon thunderstorms were forecasted. Ditto had been gone two nights and I had looked everywhere for her. I couldn't stand the thought of her being outside in a storm, maybe injured. Or trapped. The one place I hadn't searched was the junkyard. I stood by the gate trembling with indecision to enter, my hand on the phone in my jeans pocket. The posted *no trespassing* signs hung on the barbed wire fence that encircled the junkyard. So technically, I would violate privacy if I crossed onto Antree's land. A persistent queasiness nagged me with the thought of venturing any further. That's when I heard her faint meow from somewhere beyond… inside the junkyard. A meow that said *help*.

The lock on the gate proved useless since I easily scaled the barrier and landed with both feet on the other side. The smell of putrid decay accompanied my every tentative step. I wound through a dirt and weed-packed pathway lined with wrecked trucks and trailers. Past the bulldozer Antree used to arrange his trash collection of behemoths like so much furniture.

The sun disappeared behind thick, grey clouds and the day grew dark. The wind picked up and I berated myself for leaving my jacket at home. I called out Ditto's name, which is the one word I knew she understood, always drawing her from what-ever under-shed or garbage can lid location she had enthroned herself.

The circuitous path I followed became more difficult to wade through. Tall weeds, fallen tree limbs, and metal junk covered the landscape in all directions. I battled a growing sense of being lost. I called her name again, expecting to be met by my bouncing cat with a carefree expression, dispelling my over-exaggerated concerns. I trudged on, calling and listening for a clue to her whereabouts. The deeper I went, the more the feeling of being swallowed up sunk in.

A single-wide mobile home, contorted and rusted with most of the window glass gone, obstructed a portion of the pathway. In the rising breeze, I shivered and imagined the surviving kin of the animal bones huddled inside, peering out. I hurried on.

Soon, through a gauntlet of craggy oaks and overgrown sumac, I spotted a clearing to the left. A ring of rocks and metal debris circled charred remnants of a previous fire. Tucked between two blackened stones, lay an object that at first appeared to be a snake. On closer look a Coach purse covered in a slurry of ash lay empty in the dust. It struck me as an oddity to find a designer handbag discarded amongst the industrial waste.

The rumble of distant thunder convinced me to surrender the search for the time being. I turned to retrace my steps. A rustling from the scraggly underbrush startled me. Parting grasses not caused by the growing wind. I held my breath. Ditto popped through the weeds.

I blew out a breath of relief. "Where have you been, naughty cat?"

She sauntered up to me and rubbed against my leg. I petted her, checking for any injuries, but she seemed fine except for a few cockleburs that clung to her fur.

"Let's get out of here," I said trying to squelch the rising unease.

Ditto followed me keeping up with my hurried pace. My steps crunched on more bones mixed with the dirt that littered the path. I stopped to gather my bearings when the narrow trail grew confusing. Ditto walked around, looking here and there as if she too had forgotten the way out. She sat on her haunches and gave me her knowing look. Knowing what?

A broken old Pontiac leaned next to a stack of rusted scaffolding. Its cracked windshield covered with grime, etched into the surfaces.

Ditto refused to move.

"Come here, you stubborn cat." My impatience churned together with a strong desire to keep moving and I reached out to pick her up. Instead, I recoiled in disgust. A set of three ribs attached to a fragment of what looked like backbone, lay in the overgrown vegetation opposite the vehicle. Maybe from a larger animal, perhaps a deer. Scraps of hide and muscle clung to it. I suppressed a gag.

Ditto walked up and sat before me with her head cocked. Another clap of thunder boomed. This time closer than before. Sprinkles of rain began to fall.

What the hell was I doing, snooping around my neighbor's creepy property, chasing a misbehaving cat with a storm coming?

I more than once startled at some out of place movement, a scratching in the far periphery of my vision. My imagination filled with ghosts of the lives of the people who operated those cars and machines. Darting my eyes every which way only revealed the large and growing beast of my own imagination. The detritus around me murmured and creaked with the prowling of creatures of the night. Coyotes yapped in the distance. I pulled my shirt collar up against the damp chill.

The old Pontiac had no doubt been entrenched beneath the dead gray tree for years. Ditto sat by the car's slack front tire. Weary of her disobedience, I barked my demand. "Ditto, let's go now." I trotted back over the path in hopes she'd follow. Again, she refused to move.

A familiar sound of a distant motor came from the direction of the highway.

"Come on, cat, we gotta get out of here." Ditto stood. I turned to leave but whirled back around at the sound of a thump on metal. Instead of following along behind me, she had jumped up onto the hood the car. No amount of pleading could convince her to come to me. The chugging of the truck grew closer. Definitely Antree's old beater truck.

My nerves were as tight as a high wire. Lightening flashed and split the darkness for a second. Ditto stood on the hood of the car, pawing at the opaque windshield. Thunder crashed.

Curiosity got the better of me and I removed my phone from my pocket, tapping the flashlight app. I wiped my sleeve across the glass and peered into the vehicle's window.

I blinked and blinked again. Were those knuckles of hands gripping the steering wheel? A heavy shiver quaked through me. I jerked back as if burned. But I steeled myself – I had to look. Like a gawker at a house fire. A vague outline of a fist — two fists—holding to the steering wheel.

My entire body shook with fear. Legs tightened and prepared to sprint away. Instead, I steeled myself. I had to make sure it wasn't my imagination. Like a gawker at a house fire. And there … a shadowy form of a corpse tied to the steering wheel with wire. I couldn't tell for sure if it was a girl or a small man with longish hair. The head rested against the steering wheel, hiding the face. I spun away, sickness rising in my chest. Every muscle became infused with energy and I ran blindly through the rain.

Ditto caught up to me and yowled. I kept running. Ditto raced alongside me. So engrossed in the horror of what I'd just found, I had, until that moment, missed the sounds of the gate opening, the roar of the truck and its broken muffler. Now it became obvious. I stopped in my tracks, breathing in gasping gulps.

Ditto veered off the path left. Antree's truck was so close I was sure he'd seen me. I followed the cat and ducked into the underbrush behind an excavator, shivering with fear and cold. Antree motored by as if on a Sunday afternoon drive, apparently unaware.

He pulled a trailer with a Jeep chained atop the flatbed.

Inside the vehicle looked like a figure of a person in the front seat, behind the wheel. Was it my fear and imagination? Was I going crazy?

Ditto took off. I followed her, dodging behind steel barrels, galloping past the mobile home. Clambering around another three derelict cars. Past a stripped-down delivery truck, lettering long since worn away.

A short haphazard array of scrap iron pipe lay in my escape path and brought me down hard on all fours. I winced from the pain, suppressing a scream. Scrambling forward and fueled by adrenaline, I tried to ignore the throbbing in my left wrist.

Soon, we reached the beaten-down barbed-wire property line fence. Using one hand as best as I could, I managed to climb over. Ditto waited for me on the other side. We raced to the house through the rain now driving hard against my face. I barreled inside the house and locked the door. Ditto shook the off the wetness and curled into her bed, licking her paws. I pulled my phone from my pocket and dialed 9-1-1.

***

The police arrived before Antree had left. They handcuffed him and loaded him in one of the squad cars.

Police found two bodies that night and suspected at least seven more.

The cops paired them up, one by one, with long-missing persons and homicides across Southeast Iowa. Harold, Antree's occasional helper, agreed to provide testimony of his suspicions, but was not charged with any crime.

Antree, bail denied, spent the last few days of his life incarcerated. He died long before his trial. The official report cited natural causes. I read about it in the doctor's office, getting my cast on my wrist removed.

***

The winter melted away in the warming sun and with spring came the emergence of new growth, daffodils and delicate crocus, and the freshening memory of Luke. For the first time since his passing, I felt secure. Eating lunches on the deck, imagining his content presence sitting there across from me.

Ditto began making unusual faces, new expressions and meowing, I didn't know, hadn't yet learned. One day she brought home another gift. Not a mouse or squirrel. This time a very young, yellow tabby male followed her home. Another stray had found his way into our hearts. They curled up together on our deck and I named him Luke. I knew all was well again with my world.

Echoes of Revenge

Deb Miller

My name is Doctor Lily Wilson. I'm the curator at a central Alabama tourist attraction called The Southern Era Living History Plantation.

I'm also endowed with an extra sensory capability called psychometric ability. This ability has been a curse and a blessing in a profession like mine. I don't understand the science but objects, like a pottery shard, absorb and radiate their histories. Human emotions seem to do most of the imprinting when an item is being made or received as an honor. If it's a common cooking vessel, there is typically no sensory information to gather from it.

Early in life, I learned not to share this capability. People think you're insane and take nothing you say seriously. But if I use a psychometric impression to search for additional substantiating evidence, then my ability saves me a lot of time. Over my career, I've built up a reputation for having insight into ancient cultures. I've worked at some top-rated museums like the Chicago Field Museum and the Smithsonian. Teaching future generations of archaeologist at prestigious universities was gratifying. Now, however, as I approach retirement, I am fulfilled by overhauling sleepy historical sites. It's fun to excite local folks into volunteering to build attractions for everyone to enjoy and be proud of. Which is why I'm working to invigorate the Southern Era Living History Plantation.

Most days, I'm dressed in jeans, a T-shirt and hiking boots. On that warm, partly sunny morning, when the horror began, I was wearing the attire of an antebellum plantation owner's wife. When I get a chance, I love guiding tourists around our site. That day, a volunteer was not able to come, so I had the chance to take their place. That's what I was doing when Amanda, our student intern, started screaming.

She was digging in the slave cemetery's seven-foot-deep archaeological pit, while I was on the second floor of the plantation mansion. Excusing myself from the alarmed middle-aged parents and two teen girls, I hustled and rustled my full skirt onto the exterior balcony.

Amanda was running up the dirt ramp out of the pit, stumbling and screaming. Hastening down the balcony stairs to the yard and trying mightily not to step on a hem; I ran across the lawn to intercept her. She was heading towards a mobile home-sized chicken house. It's not really a chicken house. It's our disguised staff dressing rooms, the break room, and my office.

"Amanda," I called out.

She was unable to hear me shouting over her own screaming. Arriving at one of the hen house windows, she attempted to shade her face with her hands. Spinning around suddenly, she exclaimed, "I need a mirror."

She looked straight at me as I approached, but I didn't see recognition. Without waiting for me, she quickly bolted around to the back side of the hen house, where we'd hidden the structure's actual door out of the sight of tourists. I followed her inside. She stopped before the bathroom sink. As she stared at her reflection, her fingers on both hands explored her entire face.

Her eyes found mine in the mirror. "I don't understand. It bit my whole cheek off. Blood was all down my shirt. My fingers touched my teeth through the hole." Her hands gripped the sides of the sink, keeping her standing while she shook.

"Let's sit down in the break room," I said.

Taking her upper arm, I escorted her to a metal folding chair. After buying her a Dr. Pepper from the vending machine, I sat across the six-foot-long folding table from her and forced the bell-shaped skirt under it.

"Can you start from the beginning and tell me what happened?" I asked.

She said she was working on grave eight. "I'd excavated down to the body and detected a stinging odor different from the other graves I've completed. Like ammonia, you know? But not ammonia. I wanted to make an accurate description for my field notes. So, I leaned close to the skull, closed my eyes, took a big, long sniff, and held it. You know, to better describe it."

By relaying so many details, I realized the poor girl feared being accused of doing something wrong and wanted my approval. So, I nodded.

She continued, "When I opened my eyes, I was looking into the mouth of a demon. It lunged and bit my left cheek off."

All of her comments were visual, so I asked, "Did it hurt?"

"Yes. It was awful. I've never experienced such agony. My cheek was gone. I freaked out."

Pain, sounds, smells, touch were not senses I ever experience with my psychometric ability. Normally I only get visual and emotional impressions. I had expected her answer to be 'no pain'. What had Amanda experienced? Definitely more than a psychometric vision. What might have been the cause of it? A chemical? What gave off an abrasive odor? Probably a vapor rather than just an odor. I needed to smell it for myself.

"Amanda, I'm going to change out of this costume. Wait here, please. When I return, I want you to take me to the grave."

Amanda stood suddenly, flipping her chair onto its back with a clatter. Her face contorted with panic and revulsion.

"No. Please. I can't go back there."

"Calm down," I said with the tone you use for a skittish horse. "Sit down. Drink your soda. While I'm away, perhaps you can consider a method to guide me to the right location without accompanying me into the pit? Can you do that?"

"I'm sorry Dr. Wilson." She said, picking up her folding chair. "This injury," she gently touched her cheek, "has caused a horror I have never experienced before."

At the door, I watched her sit down. "It takes a while for your body to flush emotional chemicals. Please think about puppies or butterflies. Let your emotions diminish while you wait for me. I'll be back in a minute."

When I returned to the break room, she was gone.

Hurrying outside, I rounded the chicken house corner and spotted Amanda standing a few feet back from the cemetery pit. She looked visually relieved when I appeared.

Amanda said. "I couldn't just sit there. I hope you're not mad at me. I had an idea, and I wanted to see if I could direct you from the rim. I think I can."

"I'm not mad at you. But, oh my, you did give me a fright."

Her cheeks reddened. Before she could make eye contact with me, I looked into the cemetery excavation.

The pit looked odd to most of our tourists but was becoming standard for most digs. Today's archaeological excavations start by using ground penetrating radar, GPR, to locate buried objects. At the plantation, we were aware based on our scans that it was safe to remove the top four feet of dirt with a front-end loader. After that, we mark the corners of the graves with little yellow flags. Finally, we use a backhoe to take out the remaining three feet of dirt between each grave. We assign one or more archaeologists to work meticulously on each pedestal, using hand tools until they process the contents. This summer, we planned to uncover twelve burials from the much larger slave cemetery. That might not be possible now if some danger-ous substance was in some of the graves.

Amanda looked at the gas mask I was carrying. In just a few seconds, her expression went from anxiety to embarrassment. "It was a hallucination, wasn't it?"

"I have no idea what it was," I said. "But I don't think it was supernatural. Do you?"

She tilted her head to look down at the grass between us. "No, ma'am."

"Good," I said. "But something caused you to have a power-ful illusion. I'm worried it might be toxic. We need to wear protection equipment if we want to continue our investigation. This is my personal mask. There is another mask in the artifact lab I'd like you to use. I also want you to glove up until we understand what we're dealing with."

Descending the dirt ramp into the pit, I heard a movement behind me. It was Amanda, of course. She walked past, saying, "It's this way."

She made me incredibly proud of her. I was aware of her sharp intellect, but now I also discovered her courage. She had overcome the fear of her traumatic experience.

After a brief journey through the pedestals, I donned my mask and knelt by the partially exhumed skeleton of grave eight. A necklace of claws, beads, fangs, and a snake-skin bag encircled the neck and lay upon the front of a rotted cloth shirt or dress. Probably a voodoo or native African medicine neck-lace. Rituals in the American South often included candles, herbs, salt, tobacco, raptor feathers, alligator teeth, and the like. It was no surprise to find a medicine necklace such as this one.

From years of archeological experience, I know what limited psychometric effects to expect from artifacts. While reviewing the choices before me, I could tell some of them belonged to a woman. Making a selection, my fingertips brush a folded disintegrating blanket lying next to her hip.

A silent movie flickered in my mind. It came through the blanket owner's eyes. In her arms, the blanket wrapped a baby. The infant could have been around three or four months old. The mother gave its nose a quick tap, and the child looked into her eyes and gave her an open-mouthed smile. I felt the love and joy of the mother. The mother's eyes lifted from the child's face to the simple table altar at the front of the room upon which stood a one-foot crucifix. The mother experienced thankfulness and joy during her Sunday worship service.

As I removed my fingertips from the blanket, I said, "We may learn that our person was buried with a voodoo ritual, but she also attended this plantation's Christian church for the slaves."

"How do you know that?" asked Amanda.

From years of evading that question, I quickly answered. Pointing to the brick ruin next to the pit, I said, "This slave cemetery belongs to that Christian church over there. She shouldn't have been buried here unless she was a church member. Also," I added, "this small blanket buried with her must be her child's."

I almost laughed at Amanda's impressed and incredulous expression. I'll bet she thought I was Sherlock Holmes. It was a good thing I was still wearing my gas mask. It hid my 'felon's smile'.

I reached to touch the medicine necklace. Upon contacting it, the pain of a burning coal made me jerk back with a yelp.

"What is it?" asked Amanda.

I looked at my fingertip. "Wow, that was hot."

"Are you okay?"

"Yeah," I said, examining my fingertip. Anything having to do with the sense of touch: texture, heat, or pain had never been part of my psychometric sense. I considered the possibility that some strong chemical or toxin might be present. But why would anyone apply such a hallucinogenic to their necklace?

"I don't see any burn," I said to Amanda, holding up my finger. "It was probably an illusion, but it really hurt, so I'm not doing that again."

While I was looking at my remaining choices, I said, "I'm going to touch this wooden toy dog instead."

I felt no pain and exhaled a breath I wasn't aware I was holding. Again, a silent movie began. This one of despair and grief. A cruel-faced, middle-aged white man pulled loose a black boy from his mother's desperate hug. With a powerful slap, he knocked her to the ground. She scrambled to her feet to see her son striking the man face, ear, and neck with the toy dog's four legs. The man eventually caught the child's rapidly moving arm. Once he had the toy, the man hurled it into a nearby tobacco field. Focused solely on her boy, the mother fought to break free from an unseen grip holding her in place. Still watching the scene through the mother's eyes, I witnessed the slave master passing the boy to a black man inside a wagon with other slaves. The crying child clung to the slave. The slave fixed his eyes upon the mother with affection. The vision ended as the wagon drove away.

I lifted my finger from the toy dog. A tear dampened the inside of my mask. I said to Amanda, "I think this poor woman had both her husband and son sold off on the same day. At least that is how I interpret the hallucination I had."

Amanda said, "That's a terrible illusion."

"I still don't understand," I said, "why you and I are experiencing pain with some of the hallucinations and yet when I touch this toy dog, I sense nothing."

Amanda looked thoughtful. "Since you wore a gas mask for both item touches, perhaps we can conclude that the caustic smell and your gas mask have no relevance in triggering or preventing either type of episodes."

I nodded. "You're right." I stood up and brushed the dirt off my jeans. "It's frustrating, because we also don't have a clue whether these hallucinations are true or figments of our imaginations." I removed my mask.

She tipped her head to the side and asked, "how can they ever be anything but fiction?"

My psychometric ability had tripped me up again. How could I fix this stumble?

I said, "Perhaps our inductive reasoning and intuition help us understand observable background evidence that we don't realize we are seeing."

One of her eyebrows rose.

Yeah, my rationale sounded pretty lame to me, too. Shrugging, I said, "I don't know. Anyway, I'm going to call the county field service to have someone come out and test the contents of this grave. Perhaps there is a toxic substance we both absorbed, and that will explain everything. Meanwhile, let's continue using the masks and gloves." Turning to leave, I added, "Do you think you can start working on grave nine?"

Amanda said, "Once I put on my own personal protection equipment, I'll give it a whirl. If you hear me screaming, then my answer is no."

I called in my soil tests to the hazmat field service, dressed in my costume, returned to the mansion, and didn't hear another scream all day.

That night, after the plantation closed and everyone left, I changed back into my jeans. Walking to the two-lane highway. I found the front gate padlocked and the closed sign in place. Good. It was time for my in-depth investigation of grave eight. Glancing west, I noted only a half hour of daylight remained, but darkness wouldn't affect my survey.

Back at the top of the pit ramp, I looked over the entire set of pedestals. Twilight lengthened and darkened their surrounding shadows, leaving me unable to see the pit bottom. It annoyed me that I was spooked enough to want to leave my investigation until daylight. Today's events had unsettled me more than I realized. Get a grip. Nothing was going to bite my cheek off.

I put on my mask and secured a headlamp and started down. My breath was loud in my ears as I threaded my way through the pedestals in the darkness. At grave eight, I walked around its partially exhumed remains. Five inches of dirt covered the legs of the skeleton like a blanket. The head and torso lay exposed an additional ten inches, making it look like it rested on a table. As I walked, I shined the light on the woman's remains. Several objects glinted in the lamp. I intended to touch the voodoo necklace again as the final step, in addition to a button, a small jar, and a metal thimble on one of the skeletal fingers.

From my front jean pocket, I withdrew a latex glove. It would probably block my psychometric ability, but I wanted to prevent a chemical hallucination this evening if possible.

Today's powerful experience evoked a heightened sense of realism, akin to a stage play. But as I'd learned, immersion into virtual reality resulted in fantasy, the opposite of a true historic event. I needed to practice separating reality from nightmares.

First off, my vision of her family being sold manifested the normal intensity of psychometric vision without sound, verbal thoughts or words. Just emotions. My toy dog touch echoed genuine history. On the other hand, how was it possible for me to believe that the necklace was burning me like a hot coal? I had never experienced anything similar before. There had to be a chemical cause for the source of the pain and hallucinations.

Time to touch something. I chose the thimble. Nothing. I touched the jar. Nothing. Then the toy dog again. Nothing. Fine. Off with the glove.

I touched the thimble and entered a world of sounds and inner thoughts. Great. This meant I was hallucinating from the chemical. A slave woman filled with hatred embroidered beautiful red roses; brown, draft horses; and Mallard ducks into a large quilt. With each stitch of her sewing needle, the woman spoke a curse. She bonded the quilt with its future owner. The owner would be obsessed with the quilt and have horrific nightmares sleeping under it. I heard her inner thoughts of pleasure. She'd a brilliant idea for retribution, she did. She laughed. I was able to sense the joy she felt, knowing she had a solution for revenge. Those evil slavers would remain unaware she was the one causing their sleepless nights. Their feelings of guilt. A longing for death. Sewing and chanting, she laughed again.

She turned toward me and I was able to see her voodoo medicine necklace. She became aware of me and smiled. While she sewed, she chanted another curse into each quilt panel, decoration, and seam.

Since she was aware of me, I said, "Your name is Juba."

She nodded with a big smile. I watched her fangs lengthening.

"Juba, you are not real. I'm having a chemically induced hallucination." I saw myself through her eyes. This might be an illusion, but I wanted it to stop. How long would it last? I had on my gas mask. Where were my gloves?

"Oh, master, you never leaving Juba. You mine now." She split the quiet of the night with an insane cackle of glee.

I didn't believe that. I couldn't believe it. All I had to do was remove the toxin from my proximity. It was possible for me to prevent this by walking away. I hoped. But before I did that, I wanted to stop Juba's suffering. I had never believed in ghosts or the supernatural. Did I believe now? Maybe. It certainly appeared genuine. Just in case Juba's ghost was real, I'd make an attempt to free her from her own hell.

"Juba," I said, "there is no slavery now. I have no information about the location of the slave owners. However, you are aware that your son is in heaven. Right? You know that. So is your husband."

"Your magic is powerful. I am aware of that. So is your need for revenge. But surely your love for your family and friends is greater? It's time to go to them. You're not torturing slave owners anymore. You're only torturing yourself."

She stopped her sewing and chanting of curses. I sensed her strong emotional yearning for her family. She closed her eyes and there was only blackness. I was unable to sense her world anymore. Then I lost the sense of her spirit. After that I saw only her bones. She was gone.

I'm not one to rush into danger. Yet, I needed to touch her thimble again. I had to know what would happen. Would it be a typical psychometric experience, or would I descend into another chemical nightmare?

I touched the thimble. I saw a vision of a slave woman sewing and saw her mouth moving. I perceived the strong emotions of her hatred and anger. It was a typical psychometric vision. If there was no such thing as life after death, I'm sure I'd have experienced another bout of chemical toxic poisoning. That settled the matter for me. There are ghosts. How about that?

Removing my mask, I gazed at the skeleton. Rest in peace, Juba. Then I went home to do the same.

Gold Fever

Joann Schissel

Calvin retrieved the wanted poster from his saddlebag and admired his likeness. The drawing gave him a tough look with the squint of his eyes and the sharp angles of his chin and cheeks. He sounded out the words bank robbery written underneath the drawing. Reading and writing had held no interest for him growing up in the back woods. But he had learned enough to recognize the scratching that meant how much money a bounty hunter would get for turning him in. $500 Reward.

The heist had brought him less than half that amount. When the cringing bank teller refused to fork over more cash from the drawer, a murderous rage possessed Calvin's trigger finger. Just before his escape, he shot the man in the chest.

A posse had trailed him the last few days, judging by the distant cloud of swirling dust that followed off and on like a ghost. Running from the law had become commonplace in the last few years. One day his luck would change. He would find a motherlode out there. When it came, he'd hightail it to Denver, maybe San Francisco. Live the high life. Whiskey and women every night. The same things his Pappy chased before he died.

The desert rocks of the Arizona territory provided few hiding places within their crevices. He grew tired of sleepless days and nights among the cactus and sagebrush. Weary of the taste of hardtack washed down his parched throat by the few remaining drops of water in his canteen.

His horse plodded along, head down, at a pace slower than a lazy dog. Calvin reined in the mare and dismounted under a scrub tree at the top of a rise. A small cabin, maybe a couple of miles away, squatted on the low land like a dark stain on a platter of sand and prickly pear. He narrowed his eyes, sharpening his focus. Smoke curled up from the chimney. A few goats and a cow milled about in a fenced barnyard.

He waited until the sun hovered low enough in the western sky to touch the top of the distant mountain before he mounted up, slapping the animal's hindquarters with the reins. The heat of the day cooled as he weaved through the tall Saguaro. Nearing the house, the aroma of something cooking set his stomach growling.

***

Weathered wood planks on the front porch creaked under his boots. Calvin crept up to the closed door and peered through a small, dust-caked window. Inside, an old woman hunched over a caldron that hung in the fireplace. A low flame glowed underneath the iron pot, casting shadows within the room.

She straightened and looked over her shoulder. "Might as well come in, stranger. I've got vittles and a pistol. Up to you which one you want in your gut."

Calvin pulled the door open and strode in, searching the dark corners for signs of anyone lurking. Only the old woman stood before him, her frail shape silhouetted by light from the fireplace.

"Leave your sidearm at the door, she said."

The aroma of roasting meat set his mouth watering. He hung the gun belt on the hook.

The woman smoothed her gray hair back from her wrinkled face. She rubbed her eyes and her stoney expression melted into a mix of surprise and joy.

"Joey, where you been?" Your daddy and me missed you somethin' awful."

My name ain't Joey, he started to say but stopped. *She thinks I'm her son*. Before Calvin could muster any kind of response, the woman rushed up and embraced him with a hug tighter than a harness on a fat mule.

"Sit yourself down and have some grub–you must be hungry. I been expectin' you and made your favorite stew."

She motioned toward two rickety chairs next to a wood table.

Calvin seated himself. He slurped up the hot meal she placed in front of him, dipping cornbread into a steaming broth of onions, mushrooms, and goat meat.

She sat across from him and watched as he devoured the food. Her eyes glistened, reflecting the flickering tongue of light from the lantern on the table.

When he finished filling his belly, he wiped his mouth and pushed the bowl away without comment. Looking around, he took mental notes of any valuables in view. The shack held nothing worth stealing, other than a rifle that hung above the fireplace. Maybe the thin gold ring on her finger.

The woman's eyes brimmed with tears, and she dabbed her cheek. "Me and your daddy been hopin' and prayin' you'd come back, son. He told me you'd be coming home. I've been so lonely since he left." She leaned closer and lowered her voice to a whisper. "Daddy talks to me at night. Sometimes he's outside by the barn. Sometimes by my bed when I'm asleep. But when I open my eyes, he's gone."

Calvin smirked with wicked satisfaction. The old biddy was crazy as a bat. He could use her delusion to his advantage and play on her sympathy.

"Ma, you got any money here? How 'bout a good horse?"

She raised her chin. "I gots what I need for scratchin' a living. Now that you're here son, all them dark ghosts will disappear. We can bring the ranch back."

Calvin studied her meandering eyes. A madwoman, touched by too much sun. Talk of ghosts and whispers from an absent husband. Daft enough to believe him to be her long-lost son. He'd seen it before. His own crazed mama put a gun to her head when he still wore knickers.

The old crone will be an easy mark. He'd hole up long enough to hide out from the posse and rest his horse. He'd take what he pleased and send the old woman to her maker with a twist of her scrawny neck. Not a soul left to tell tales about his whereabouts.

"Ma," he said raising his voice. "Where's your money?"

The old woman just shook her head. "Ain't got no money. Only a couple rocks Daddy pulled from a cave in the mountain."

Calvin perked up. "Rocks? Gold rocks?"

She nodded. "Daddy told me to keep 'em for tradin'.

Calvin's pulse quickened. "Where? Let me see them."

She shuffled over to the fireplace, removed a tin box from the mantle, and placed it in front of him. "Go on, open it."

He reached inside and pulled out a rock the size of his palm. Gold crystals gleamed in the veins.

"There's more, too," she said and took a step away.

Calvin wanted to spring to his feet and dance a jig. Excitement ballooned in his head and his body quivered with delight. But he kept a poker face.

"When's Daddy coming back?" Sweat beaded along his scalp. He didn't want any unexpected company to interrupt his dream come true.

She shook her head. "Don't rightly know. He just turned up gone last spring. He got the gold fever somethin' fierce. Said he was goin' to the mountain. Hitched up Nelly to the wagon and that's the last I seen of him … waving goodbye with the kerchief I made for him. The muslin one with the red heart embroidered on it." Her face held a faraway expression. "Promised he'd be back."

Calvin couldn't concentrate on her rambling. His mind spun in a blur.

"Take me to the gold," he said in a voice that rattled and echoed around in his head.

His skin burned hot and cold with sweat and shivers. The thought of riches sent his heart thumping so loud he could hear it. Real as the Native ceremonial drums carried on the dusty breeze.

Ma's face pinched. "Best let it be. The fever can take your soul and leave nothin' but sorrow."

"Well, now, Ma, I insist." Calvin placed his hand on his empty hip where his six-shooter usually hung. He'd need it later, but for the time being, he just smiled with false sweetness.

She ambled to the door. Her bony finger beckoned him to follow her outside.

Moonlight bathed their path across the billowing sand. Stars peppered the ebony sky brighter than he'd ever seen, like they could burst into a dazzling firework at any minute.

They trudged toward the barn. Ma held the lantern straight out at her side and its beam swayed back and forth with each footstep in a mesmerizing tempo.

Stirred-up sand blew grit into his eyes and nose. An abrupt wave of dizziness seized him, and his steps faltered. His body reeled without control. Muscles strummed like strings, plucked by invisible fingers.

"What's wrong?" she asked. "You look a might peaked." Her hair glinted silver in the churning wind and haloed around her, each leaping strand a writhing snake-like creature. Stars in the heavens wobbled like excited fireflies in all colors of the rainbow.

He choked as if an unseen hand had tightened around his throat. Air escaped from his lungs. "You some kind of skin-walker? What's this black magic?" His voice wavered, and he clawed his neck. "You've poisoned me." His wild eyes locked on hers.

She cackled and her flesh rippled across her face in waves. Teeth flashed sharp as white daggers.

"I'm just an old woman. It's them wicked spirits you should fear, not me. It's the stew, don't you see? My special mushrooms opens up what you got inside. Brings out them tormented demons straight from hell."

Bloody tears trailed down her cheeks and seared into her flesh, only to disappear the next moment. Her mouth contorted and she expelled a low bestial groan. "You were a bad boy for running away from us, Joey."

She turned away from him. The lantern's yellow glow spiraled around her in a narrow ring of shimmering light, swirling against the black sky.

He stumbled behind her like a clinging toddler, pulled by a magnetic force that leashed him to the hem of her skirt.

***

A root cellar door appeared at his feet, slung low and horizontal, protruding from the ground like an ancient tomb. Its timbered door squeaked open by an invisible force, revealing a black hole.

Ma deposited the lantern into the earthen cavity and stepped aside, pointing downward.

Calvin fell to his knees and crawled to its entrance. A shiver coursed through him when he gazed into what lay strewn across the dirt floor inside. It sparkled with brilliance, like sunlight on waves, dazzling in its beauty. Blinding with hypnotic hold. Unmistakable. Gold. Bags of it.

"Do you see it, boy?" she cried out through the blustering wind. "It's yours. Take it. All that evil metal has only caused death and misery. I'll not touch it again for fear of my mortal soul."

A thrumming sound rumbled from above. Hushed at first, it grew into a deafening hum of voices. Hundreds of them. High-pitched screeching roared. He clamped the palm of his hands over his ears. The smell of sulfur, hot and sickening, strangled him. Black shapes barreled in from all directions and pecked his head and neck. He flailed his arms, thrashing the air with uncontrolled punches. The beating of devil wings tore at his face and hands, ripping pieces of his flesh in a frenzy. Torrents of pain burned through his body.

He stumbled, blinded by what he couldn't comprehend. The gold became his singular thought. Calling to him. He hurled himself into the bowels of the dirt and rock-lined cellar.

Ma screamed into the gale. She retrieved a pistol from her skirt and waved it in the air. "They're coming for you, Joey! I see them ghost riders bearing down. Don't leave me again, boy. Stay here with us."

Above him, the cellar door slammed shut with a thunderous boom. The sound of a bolt scraped across its timbers.

Tears streamed down his cheeks and terror shook his body. Dizzy and weak, his arms and legs became ponderous weights.

The gold whispered to him with a seductive voice, and he caressed the nuggets like a lover. The flame of the lantern began to flicker lower.

His head rolled to the side, and he gasped for breath.

Just before the lantern's wick extinguished, its fading light disclosed a scrap of muslin embroidered with a red heart. The handkerchief encircled the neck of a gray, withered corpse. Its decayed skull bore a skeletal grimace, mocking their shared fate.

Calvin's heart slowed, then it stopped. The gold kissed his lips and stole his last breath.

Middle Ground

Michael Van Natta

Hal Michaels was one week new to the room, although time seemed to have no meaning now. He faced ten other men across a large oval conference table. He'd been dealt his cards here and held them up, pairing up suits, rearranging strategy. That he was forgetting something nagged at him, the details he couldn't quite remember. That game was over now, or so he'd been told.

Before all this started, he'd never played Bridge and never would have, had it not been for the woman. What he'd done. He was guilty, of what, he couldn't quite remember.

The exact rules of Bridge had never been explained so he was learning as he went. The focus seemed to be on "getting out," as Williamson, his playing partner had told him. Williamson had longish hair that hid a brown birthmark patch at his hairline. He'd had been in the room for "a couple of years."

The room was round and washed with a subtle smell of moss and stagnant water. No real windows, but two windowed doors. It felt a little like the holding room at the 10th Street jail, a place he'd been once when he was thirty and thirsty. Or was he eighteen? Or maybe it was while he was somewhere overseas. He didn't remember exactly. Come to think of it, maybe the jail thing was a figment of his imagination.

The walls were solid but cracked plaster and water stains gave them a scabrous feel, with prints of renaissance paintings of Hieronymus Bosch's visions of damnation alternating with Michelangelo's more heavenly works. A framed sign hung on one wall that said in ornate silver calligraphy, "Bridge Room." There was no refrigerator, no stove, sink or cabinets and no beds. No clock.

Wondrous and baffling. Hal hadn't a clue why, but he never felt the need to sleep, to eat or drink. It seemed to him that bodily functions no longer mattered. New rules here.

He's been told one door led through a hall to the office of the Overseer, Sam Betterton. Williamson called him the Warden, which always gathered a smattering of chuckles from the guys.

The other opened to a door to the "good old terra firma," as Williamson liked to refer to it. No chuckles with that one, it seemed to be a given. Through this second door ran a long hallway and then another door that supposedly opened next to the Hill Street Open Market in west Los Angeles. He didn't know. He'd hadn't left the room all week. No one had. Like his memory, time was getting away from him, becoming vague, blurred. Sleep deprivation does that, he thought. And starvation, yet he wasn't hungry or tired.

The banter was casual but focused on the card game as if heaven and earth depended on the outcome. The men were divided, about half and half. Each partnered up, save one guy of the other team who, for some reason, had no partner. Hal had never been told why. Each man wore a nice suit, including Hal, who had on his best, the Peter Ortay he'd picked up somewhere along the line. The mood was pleasant but a bit adversarial when it came to interpreting the rules of Bridge. Jovial, but underneath, a heavier darker note.

"Delbert Greenfield," one man said–Hal thought his name was Arnot or something. "Who names their kid Delbert?"

Hal chuckled. There was a lot of polite chuckling going on, as if each man knew some inglorious inside joke.

"Guy was destined, don't you think?" said Deshawn from his side. "Name like that…"

***

Betterton hung up the blue phone – the old fashioned kind with the number dial. The boss had been curt, clear and strident. Get results.

He stood, donned his duty cap, adjusted his gun belt, checked the snap over the Glock and went to one of the many doors, pushed through and walked out of the Casey's Pawn Shop on South Sunset Boulevard and into the evening smog. The hazy red sun was bouncing on the western horizon.

The surrounds had been his beat in the distant past. He knew the regulars, had taken down his share. Knew the gangs, the streets and the street people. They were always the same, year after year. The crimes the same, too. One or more of the seven. Take your pick.

He considered this "home turf," but he'd been transferred so many times, had to get to know so many cops and robbers, that his head spun in the muted west coast dusk.

He was old and no longer mattered to the world. They'd stripped him of his street duties after he'd solved the double murder in Van Nuys and they'd made him an Overseer, a fancy word for administrator. So long ago all of the details of the murder case were gone from memory.

His job was go out to observe only—he was prevented by the rules from taking any direct action—then return and coordinate a strategy to remove some specific evil of the world using his operatives in the Bridge Room. At this, he'd been good. He'd had nothing else to do for so long, he'd honed his abilities to a fine point and grown fat and out of shape doing it.

But this evil, this Portman woman, was getting away from

him. Sweat formed under his armpits in the sultry heat. He had to find a way to take her down. He was so close to the next level. He couldn't… wouldn't fail now.

He stood a minute, watching the dense traffic, the darkened windows of long black cars, the low riders and their thrumming bass speakers, the pimped-out orange or sky-blue convertibles. Detritus of decadent lives. He reached into his suit pocket and withdrew the faxed photo he got from the boss, a head shot of a woman, age 34, beautiful – even by California standards - blonde, teeth too perfect. Maybe a hint of teenage acne washed by plastic surgery. The name printed at the bottom read "Honey Portman" He gave a low whistle that caught the attention of a player-type sauntering by and waved it in front of the gaunt man's unfocused eyes. The uniform always worked. It gave him the edge. While the freak gawked, Ward read the back print matter: Just one bust for solicitation eighteen months ago. Suspicion of murder, unfounded, two years ago. So, new. Or else careful. It sent that familiar thrill of the chase through his being.

Working the street gave Betterton some much-needed reprieve from his desk job but he knew he didn't have long. The world sucked the life from him - and all his operatives - if they lingered. A couple of hours on the streets and he'd start to feel ill. It would be all but unbearable by the six hour mark. Like swimming under water. He was good though, and knew it. Efficiency was everything. Discernment. It was why he was Overseer.

"Yeah, I saw that girl a couple of nights ago, over to Lacy Babes. Hanging out front. Not one of the dancers, yo? The bitch knows how to show it off, know what I'm sayin'? What'd she do?"

Betterton re-folded the photo, put it back in his pocket, made a beeline for the Boulevard.

The junkie yelled after him. "Hey, you got a smoke, man?" Betterton ignored him. It was about efficiency.

***

Betterton sat back. He'd spent a lot of time on the street – too much. He had an accurate internal clock, sharpened by an eternity of use. Twelve hours max out there was the most anyone had suffered through and it'd taken that guy forever to recover. After six, functions began to go haywire. By eight, it hurt in the bones, by ten, you could hardly breath.

Weary, he typed out the fax on the old Smith Corona and sent it. He wished they'd allow computers – life would be so much more efficient, but they were banned.

He'd found Portman, of course. Right where the burnout said she was and followed her movements from the strip club to a small torn-up bungalow on West 121st, watched as men ogled her, approached her, stopped their cars along curbs as she cat-walked by.

She wore black tights and a thin low cut red top pinned with a broach depicting the white horse, her bare neck adorned with a matching white bow tie. A white narrow brimmed hat with a gold crown. Long sleek legs and four-inch red heels completed the picture. A red sweet necter-laden flower amid the weeds that stained the sidewalk. A Venus de Milo fly-trap open and waiting.

She never got in a vehicle. Teased them, she did. Rebuffed all approaches. So he knew. Pure blackness. Dark matter. Pride and Anger, the First Horseman, Conquest.

Nothing subtle about it. Expected.

Ten men the boss knew of had been taken off the street. Another, whereabouts unknown. Portman was suspect number one. He hadn't followed her inside the house but Betterton caught a fleeting glimpse of the eleventh man through a window at the back of the house. Yep. It was as the boss said. Indeed, it was Hal. The boss was never wrong. Never.

***

Some time later, a whirring noise came from a small table near the door. The men looked up from their cards. The idle chatter in the room ceased.

"Can you get that, Hal?" Williamson said.

Hal thought Bridge was played in partnerships but this game had different directions, a necessity with so many players, and a thing in constant flux, pausing sometimes for hours while polite arguments ensued over some arcane rule. Their own actions seemed to be under the restraint of unwritten laws, as if they were being judged by unseen others. Hal had by then checked out the windows from his seat at the table, remembering his time in the jail, but they seemed ordinary. Not mirrored two-ways.

He stood and went to the table and removed a page of paper off the fax machine. He chanced a peek through the small window mounted in the door with the sticky note that said in handwritten scrawl: "Boulevard." A long hallway lit by sconces along both walls terminated in another closed door.

"Ah, here it is," Williamson said when Hal handed him the fax. Murmurs rose all around. Men set their cards face down on the table, leaned forward or sat back. Everyone waited on Williamson, who took his damn time but then smiled broadly and looked about.

"Finally," he said. "Here it is."

More clearing of throats, pursing of lips.

"Hal?" Williamson said. "Are you up to it?"

Hal looked around, suddenly the center of attention.

"Up to what?" This was all new to him.

"We're all counting on you," Armon said from across the table.

"Our last remaining shot," another said.

"What?" Hal asked again.

***

The game had been put on hold. A few minutes went by. Or maybe a month, who knows? Time didn't matter here. No doubt the men would all go back to it once Hal walked out the door.

They each shook his hand, offered some friendly advice from their own experience. A couple of men on his team clapped his back. Hal did his best and tried to not let on how freaked out he was, how fucked up this all was. The instructions were vague, like everything else. He put on his best macho act, hesitating as long as he dared, but he knew they saw through it all. They all had been there, where he was heading. He understood as much. They'd all done something like what he was tasked to do.

"You got this, man," Williamson said. His face looked haggard.

"The distance thing, that's key," said Armon, adjusting Hal's tie.

"Go deep, I'd say," said a third.

Hal somehow knew they all hoped he'd be better at it than they had been.

Finally, all pep rally stuff done, all words said, all fortitude shared, Hal turned and walked through the door, through the open market and out into the heat and neon jangle of the Boulevard under a moonless sky.

Like with the weird made-up Bridge, he sensed there were

now indecipherable strange rules. And like Bridge, they'd never been sufficiently explained to him.

***

Honey Portman looked upon her man. He was asleep, maybe unconscious, one or the other. She loved him and hated him. Loved him, because he'd been so insanely attracted to her three nights ago. She could tell. He was the kind of guy that would do anything to have her. Why wasn't she happy?

She hated him, too, for what he was. She would take him down.

Portman herself was unhappily married to Jack, a soldier of fortune who was always off fighting wars somewhere. By day, she worked at Paramount Studios, Director of Talent. She didn't do the routine interviews of fledgling actors or actresses anymore. That job fell to Ms. Simpson now.

When Mr. Williamson was her boss, she had to do it all. She was good at it – maybe even a little prideful. Three of her "finds" were now on big and small screens in enduring and endearing roles. It might have been that way still, except that Mr. Williamson got hungry. It didn't matter that he had a waif of an actress ten years his junior at home, waiting on his every request, every desire. It didn't matter that he could lose everything. He had been blinded by her beauty, smitten by greed and gluttony, and rose to her presumed innocence. They all had. They were all the same. Men.

He was the first. Three years ago.

What happened to Williamson made her sick. What she'd done to him, not wanting to, but done, wasn't all her fault. She hadn't been good at it then. She'd made mistakes, had to cut corners. It was all new to her; no rules to follow. She knew she was lucky to have escaped the suspicions thrown her way.

Months went by as she thought of how it would have been better handled, she found a certain, well…pleasure in her planning. A sense of control she'd never known growing up Catholic in Cleveland. She told herself at first that it all been an accident of circumstances. She wasn't to blame. But she liked her thoughts and before she realized what she was doing, she was tempting the fates. Imagining what might happen. Fantasizing. Drinking in the poison of passion. Planning.

It had been no surprise then when a eight months later another man came along. Armon, his name was. How fitting. How utterly vainglorious. And, of course, wearing an Armani suit.

Bastards all.

***

Before Hal left on his mission through the Boulevard door, he'd been summoned down the hall and sat waiting on Betterton in the man's small office filled with filing cabinets, a big desk in front of a comfortable-looking chair. He'd taken the other, a metal folding chair, and wondered where all the many doors in the office went. After a time, he grew fidgety and paced. He noticed an old blue telephone and an old red one, a fax machine, and then, growing bolder, looked through some of the many tiny windows. Each showed long halls and the closed doors at the other end, just like the hall he'd come through.

Nothing made sense. He didn't know how he'd gotten to the room with the Bridge players. He had only vague memories of an indistinct past. One minute he was…where? And the next, playing Bridge, cards in hand, facing ten other men. Or maybe there was something? He just didn't know.

The door behind the desk opened and a large man he hadn't met barged through wearing a navy-blue police uniform, complete with duty cap, holstered black gun, handcuffs, a gold badge and he didn't know what else.

"Sit down, Michaels. I'm Betterton." the man said. His voice seemed to come over a field of gravel. "I'll get right to the point."

Hal sat and watched dumbfounded as the man took off his heavily-laden duty belt and hung it on a coat tree behind his chair, then stripped all the way down to green boxer briefs and pulled on a blue tight-fitting T-shirt that said, "Ain't Life Great?" in bold white letters across his broad muscled chest. He had a gut on him and gave off a faint smell of sweat and Irish Spring soap. Finally, he dropped into the desk chair and opened a thick folder on the blotter Hal had missed on first inspection. He pulled out an eight by ten color photo and flipped it onto the blotter before Hal.

"This," he said, tapping the glossy, "is the enemy."

The picture showed a head-shot of what looked like some Hollywood starlet, quite beautiful. He made no comment, hoping his intimidation didn't show.

"Your mission is to locate this woman and wait for our subject to show. He will, trust me. But nothing else. You got me?"

"I hear what you're saying. But how... I..."

Betterton abruptly stood. The back of the T shirt said "No Question." He grabbed a black jacket off a coat tree and tossed it across the desk. "Take off your suit coat," he said.

"What?"

"Did I stutter, Michaels? Take off your jacket."

Hal stood tentatively and began disrobing.

Once again, prison bars and clanging, walls and cots came to mind. Last week? He had a sudden memory of black uniforms, foreign tongues. Unconsciously, he reached up and touched his left shoulder.

He soon stood in shirt sleeves in front of Betterton, exposed.

"Now put that on." Hal's eyes followed the man's index finger. The jacket looked so dark as if to be made of coal. Matte finish. No light emanated from its surface, no reflections along the folds from fritzing overhead room lights. It might as well have been a hole in the universe. When he touched it, he pulled his hands back, shocked by a faint but clear vibration, a buzzing. Determined to do as told, he grabbed it and went through the motions of putting it on.

"Remain standing, Michaels."

"Yes sir."

"Now, this coat is your gait way, your 'in,' as it were. Be careful with it. It's ancient. We don't use it too often but we're at our wit's end here with this case."

Hal waited and watched Betterton fold his hands on the desk.

"How much faith do you have, Michaels?"

"Faith? I don't know what you mean, - faith."

"I told you this coat was ancient. It goes back to David and Saul. Even Joseph. You know, from the Bible?

"Ah…sorry. Don't know them."

"Never mind. Look, If I tell you that I can't see you now, would you have faith in me?"

"I… that's not something I…"

"Well, forget faith then. Just believe me when I say I can't see you. You are invisible. That's what the coat does. It's the coat of invisibility. I literally do not know if you are still standing in front of me or not."

"I believe you, sir, but how can that be? That's impossible."

"Nothing's impossible. You gotta learn to not question so much, Michaels. We're sending you out with that on. Slip it on once you're in the hallway. But once you're on the street, touch nothing. Speak not a word to anyone. Do not allow anyone to touch you. You're to have no interaction with the world except to see with your eyes, hear with your ears, smell with your nose. Got it?"

Hal nodded. "If you say so." He looked down at himself, at his chest, legs. He could clearly see them. Doubts rose even more. "If it's not that woman, then who is the subject?"

"Glad you asked. Go ahead and sit your butt back down." He removed another photo from the file and tossed it on the blotter. "This is our subject. Delbert Greenfield. Age 31. Ex-Marine, works Private Security. Divorced. Prior Domestic Abuse arrest and got community service, charges dropped after that. No children. Lonely guy and a loner by everyone's account. Turns out he's on a deadly path. Our job is to, well, turn him away from the enemy. Save his life from the evil he's toying with. Save him from himself, if you get what I'm saying."

Betterton's eyes knifed into Hal's. "Take the photo. Relevant contact information is on the back. But don't talk to him, touch him or let him know you're close by. Just observe. Then come back the way you went. Report back to me. Got it?"

Hal swallowed and nodded.

"Take the coat off now and don't put it on until you're in the hall, on the way out to the street."

Hal did as he was told.

"Now, get outta here," Betterton said.

***

Hal stepped through the door. It opened to a wide street, lit by a pale moon, overhead streetlights and a menagerie of neon signs. The air smelled of the salty ocean. A scattering of people dressed anywhere from surfer duds to skimpy shorts and halter tops on roller skates to three-piece suits stood in clusters or sauntered along the sidewalks. A few scantily-clad very young women danced on a corner in clunky four-inch heels mixed with a few nattily-attired glamor girls walking back and forth, displaying their feathers.

Vehicles of all stripes, gleaming with reflected light, cruised up and down the boulevard. Hot and thick air belied Hal's notion of a late night hour. The bars and clubs hummed with beat music filtering over the street.

He found Greenfield first, leaning against a dark door post. With is curly unruly mop and honed physique, he matched the photo. Hal walked toward him but decided first to test the theory. He smoothed his jacket and walked straight into a couple of men coming toward him. At the last moment, he ducked out of their way and they carried on, unfettered. Neither gave him the slightest notice.

He tried it again, a dude with ear buds tucked in, eyes down, head bobbing. This time, he intentionally bumped the man's shoulder on the way past, clearly violating Betterton's directions.

"Hey," the man said as Hal passed. He whipped his head left and right, confusion showing on his face, before he shrugged and carried on.

Still not convinced, he tried one last thing. He lifted up a discarded fast-food drink cup and held it in front of three women huddled in conversation. At first, they didn't notice the cup, as if such an apparition was impossible. Then they did notice it. One by one, they jumped back. One yelped, another's eyes widened. The third put her hands out as if to block the sight. Hal dropped the cup, but hovered near them as they disavowed what had just happened. Laughed at their foolish folly even before the cup came to a complete rest on the pavement. Hal became a believer.

A crushing pain blasted into his right rib cage, as if he'd been hit by a moving car. He staggered left into a wall, gripped his side. He had a vague memory of a similar pain once in his left shoulder, didn't remember more than that. It left him as soon as it had come.

None of the people passing by gave him a single look. He again thought of the rules of this world, or lack of them.

Greenfield was there still, but standing straight now. He followed the man's line of sight and saw the enemy at the curb, Portman. The movie star. She leaned next to a long white Lincoln SUV, her head almost in the window.

Greenfield stood directly behind her on the filthy sidewalk, hesitation written on his face. rocking forward toward her and then back. After a couple of minutes, the woman stood up and, paying no attention to Greenfield, walked on down the boulevard past a parade of shops that once were upscale but now catered to the less well-heeled clientèle. Greenfield followed the woman with Hal tailing behind, noting the amorous way Portman swayed her hips. He could see why the men in the room had fallen all over her. They'd never said specifically what acts they'd committed with this woman, if they even remembered.

At one point, Portman stopped to examine lingerie in a window-front. Greenfield slowed but then walked up beside her, stuck a cigarette in his mouth and motioned for a light. The woman gave him the once over, sneered and turning on her high heels, hurried away. It pissed Hal off. She's a bitch, he thought. A tease.

Greenfield pivoted and walked right past Hal without a glance, face contorted by anger and frustration. After a half block, he stopped at a small vending cart where a beaded street vendor sold nick-knacks and trinkets, cheap paste jewelry and the like. Greenfield passed some currency to the man who handed him a yellow and green two foot tall stuffed bear. As he walked on, he held the toy clutched to his chest, his other arm pumping out and back as if he was playing an invisible drum. To Hal's surprise, he turned a corner into the alley. Hal followed him around but then stopped dead in his tracks.

Greenfield had come to stand over a dented metal trash can. Holding the stuffed bear by the neck, he commenced to shaking it, almost as if he was strangling the lifeless toy. He paused only to pull out an object from his pants pocket. Hal, now standing close enough to touch him, heard a sharp click, saw a glint of metal in the weak light. Greenfield viciously stabbed the bear repeatedly with the switchblade. He grunted, sobbed softly, tears streaking across his face, snot coming from his nose. Stuffing flew up and out and down. After a flurry of jabs, Greenfield dropped the shredded toy into the trash bin. He turned and walked out of the alley.

A short while later, Greenfield, with traces of white fluff clinging to his dark hoodie, sat at a table at the Wendy's on 114th Place. The lone customer, he ate a burger and fries and downed a Coke. Hal watched him through a window from outside. When Greenfield finished, he grew animated. He flailed and banged his tray over the trash when the paper ketchup-soaked wrappers on his food tray refused to tip into bin. Hal remembered the feeling. He'd had that happen to him, too. Frustrating.

Finally, Greenfield succeeded and the debris fell away from the brown tray. He tossed into atop with the other dirty trays, turned and walked out.

Some time later through darkened side streets, Greenfield walked into a small bungalow through a garage door on Willow Walk Drive. A red corvette without a speck of dust or rain-spots took up the single bay. A chamois cloth hung from one of the rear-views.

Hal looked the place over but hadn't tried to follow when Greenfield went through the door. He feared he'd get trapped inside. Instead, he observed him through the windows.

The man lived a spartan existence, punctilious, everything

in its place. Hal waited outside, watching Greenfield go through two Coors and a half bag of chips, watching The Late Show from a black sofa. After the monologue, Greenfield turned the television off, stood and stepped through a door off the kitchen and disappeared down a set of stairs. After a time, he came back up, shut the door, walked down a hall, turning off the lights as he went.

Hal wished now he'd sneaked in with Greenfield. He found the door again, tried the knob but it was locked. He wondered if Betterton would think he'd just made a mistake.

Those guilty thoughts, some sort of dereliction of duty, still roamed his mind when he passed through the door at the market and back into the room. He hadn't gotten much on Greenfield but the man clearly had a thing for Portman. He needed to get into that basement.

***

The card game paused when he walked in. All eyes were upon him. He hung the coal-black jacket on the hook assigned him and sat at his spot next to his partner, Williamson. He was in no hurry to face Betterton.

Hal had learned things through idle conversations during the playing of the cards. Each of the men in the room had been intimately involved in the movie star's life in some way that struck Hal as unsavory and certainly disappointing when all was said and done.

They listened as Hal told his story of what he'd seen following Greenfield.

After Hal finished and all questions were answered, the game resumed. Cards were laid or flipped, or held close to the chest. The banter was light-hearted, peppered with off -color jokes. They shared, one by one, how during their time there, they'd done as he had, taking orders from Betterton; making efforts to correct the ongoing evil, trying to bring some semblance of justice to the world beyond the room. A pall of guilt and shame hung over the table like smoke in a pool hall. But also a sense of kinship, a camaraderie, colored their conversations. Each man spoke in turn or not, each confessing his own shortcomings, which, frankly, all agreed, was the reason for the game, their very existence in the room. They all talked of their hope for clemency, some mitigation, some early release to some vague notion of a better place.

Williamson had been the first and now Hal was the last. Eleven men, an odd number. Off-kilter. A crooked picture on the wall.

Two groups, each at their side of the big table, all holding cards. Three groups of partners facing off against three groups of partners - except one of the partners across the table had no partner. Greenfield, of course, was still out there.

Time past. Williamson declared a new rubber match and Arnot brought out a new deck to replace the beaten-up old cards. Murmurs of agreement filtered across the table and met in the middle.

The hope was they'd never see him, Greenfield, never have to welcome the twelfth man, never have Greenfield partnered up. That would be a disaster, would add unknowable time to the already interminable game. There was still that chance. Hal came to further see that he was their chance when the fax came in.

***

Williamson read the missive from Betterton. "He wants you to go back to Greenfield's and get in the house."

Hal felt his face color up. Williamson handed the fax to Armon, who read it silently and smiled.

"Williamson is being charitable. Get this, guys. Betterton's words …" Armon started to laugh and had to wait until he could speak again. "Betterton's words here are 'Get your ass back out there and don't come back until you know every fucking inch of that house and every fucking thought that runs through Greenfield's head.'"

Armon turned the page so everyone could see it. Hal's gut clenched up when he saw all the huge exclamation points. Hal, on an impulse, stood abruptly and grabbed the fax out of Armon's hands.

He stood and got the coat off the hook. "No sense wasting time," he said.

He went through the door marked "Overseer" to face the music. Maybe get some answers.

***

"Well, well, Michaels. I figured you'd come by before you went out again."

Hal tossed the black coat over the back of the metal chair and sat. Betterton sat behind his desk, in uniform. Flushed and sweating, he'd pulled down his tie and unbuttoned his uniform collar. An oscillating fan blew air over the desk from a corner.

"Sorry to butt in unannounced, but I have a few questions."

"Hal, I got a million questions, too. But you know the score, We don't ask. They tell."

"Should I have followed Greenfield into his house?"

"Hell yes, you should have." Betterton glared at Hal. "You were proximate, saw who he was and you had invisibility, for God's sake. We coulda been a lot farther down the road on this if you would have handled it. I've been doing this a lot longer than you. So it's back out you go. I just got back myself."

"From Greenfield's house?"

"There, and other places."

"Are you okay? You look like you're hurting, sir. What happened out there?"

Betterton waved a dismissive hand. "I know better but I tried to push it. Stayed out too long. Anyway, this Greenfield's in some real trouble."

Betterton turned his chair and spread his arms before the fan and went on.

"Here's what we know. First, Portman is accelerating. Hitting her vics faster. It's down to one every week or so. Second, the Boss thinks Greenfield is gonna be next because he's obsessed with her. Apparently, he's got some past shit, a history of ignoring danger when he's on his high horse. So we got to stop him for his own good. His very soul is in peril. Third, the only way to do that is throw some mud in his way. That's where you come in. You got to get close and somehow divert him. I think we might have you make contact."

"What's that entail?"

"It means you go in and find a way to persuade him of his predicament. And no invisibility this time."

"He'll see me?"

"You'll look like any other Joe Blow to him and try to keep it that way. But you have to carry some authority, just in case."

Betterton opened his desk drawer and pulled out a badge affixed to a leather pocket case and a small pistol wrapped in a tight leather holster and dropped them on the desk. The badge had the letters FBI prominently displayed.

"Turns out another room needs the coat. Anyway, these are all you'll need for this mission. Greenfield's not paying attention to anything but Portman lately. He's let his driver's license lapse and his car tags are out of date. So worst case, we can pick him up and take him off the scene for a few days."

"Pick him up? How do we do that? Are the local cops on to

this?

Betterton gave Hal a withering look. "The local detectives are, shall we say, benefiting from their investigation. Playing with the devil. Stay clear of them. If you have to resort to an arrest, we'll know and we'll alert some other room to bring him in."

"How..."

"Don't question, Michaels. Haven't you learned anything yet?"

Betterton leaned across the desk, looked left and right and said in a soft conspiratorial tone, "They have some of us infiltrated in the LAPD - it's a widely known secret."

He smiled as if he enjoyed giving Hal some of the inside poop.

"Also, we got a vehicle parked outside, a brown Toyota Corolla, late-model. You'll need it. And don't forget. You're completely visible now.

***

Though it felt like he'd just been gone a few minutes, when he exited out through Hill Street Market onto 120th and turned onto the Boulevard, it was early morning—rush hour was just starting—and already hot. The Toyota was where Betterton said, parked in front of a bakery. Dressed in his suit and badge secured in the front left pocket for easy access, the pocket slip holster that held the .233 Ruger felt invasive, uncomfortable over his right hip. He pulled the key fob from his left pocket and started the vehicle, flipped on the AC.

Taking the 101 north, he made some plans on the way over to Greenfield's location. His first job was to follow the man to his place of employment and not get caught doing it. All new to him, this cop stuff.

He parked and sat out along Willow Walk a few lots up from Greenfield's bungalow and across the street, tapping his fingers on the steering wheel. Cognizant he was now completely visible, he watched to be sure he wasn't noticed when the garage door went up and the red Corvette backed out and drove off the other direction.

Hal maneuvered the Toyota to stay three or four cars behind the Corvette. Traffic was thick and slow. The red car made no sudden maneuvers that he interpreted as Greenfield picking him up on the tail. Soon, Greenfield headed east and drove over the canyon ridge and the congestion eased. Hal had to be more careful then and he stayed a half mile back. There were other red cars but no other Corvettes.

He followed Greenfield all the way to a warehouse-like structure on a hundred acres of flat dusty ground where the vehicle parked and the man exited wearing a light blue security uniform. He watched him walk all the way in. He started the Toyota again and on the way out, noticed the large company sign that read "Edge Enterprises," a name, he thought, about as nondescript as possible.

Back at Greenfield's house, he parked on the street - this time in front of an empty-looking house with a For Sale sign in the yard. He walked some hundred yards to the bungalow, watching for signs of life in the other residences. He saw nothing moving.

He went around back and following his instincts checked all the likely spots and eventually found a duplicate key on top of a wooden grape trellis. He entered the back door, closed it behind him and stood in a small eating area off the kitchen. The drapes and blinds were mostly closed and the house was dark. The air gave off the sour smell of greasy fried food. He thought about how police on crime shows he may have watched—or just imagined that he'd watched—always put on latex gloves in situations like this but he'd been told they weren't necessary. He was not told the reason why but had discovered on his own that his all his fingers - and toes - lacked the usual microscopic whirls and ridges that might give him away. It was an alarming discovery that still had no answers.

The house was as orderly and clean as he'd seen before. Everything in its place, in almost military precision. He went through the cupboards and drawers, peeked in the frig and found nothing unusual. He moved to the main living room.

It was the same there. A sofa, a recliner, a coffee table, end table, television and surround sound system. A few pictures hanging on the wall that could have been found in any low-rent hotel in the city. On the end table, though, he found a framed picture of three people standing before the ocean, feet in the surf. In the middle was Greenfield, hair windblown and messy, in red swim trunks. A woman was to his left with rolled up jeans and on his right was a girl the size of a ten- year- old in a pink bathing suit. The faces of the females had been blacked out by a marker of some kind. He suddenly felt sorry for Green-field. He sensed a sadness amid his desperation.

He moved to the single bedroom. The closet held a sparse collection of men's clothing only; two additional uniform shirts, some dockers and a couple of polos. He remembered Green-field was divorced and had the domestic charge that'd been dismissed. The chest of drawers held the usual underwear and socks, T shirts and jeans. No weapons.

Next to the full-size bed on a nightstand he saw a photo of a woman and when he looked more closely, saw it was the same head shot glamor photo of Portman he'd been shown by Betterton.

The bathroom was just a bathroom. He expected to see the normal residue of bachelor life - toilet rings and hair - but like the rest of the house, the porcelain surfaced gleamed and the spotless sink displayed his Gillette razor, can of shaving cream of the same brand, a soap dispenser, a bottle of Obsession for Men, and a toothbrush and Ultrabright toothpaste in a chipped coffee mug that said "Dad" on the outside. The shower stall was likewise sparkling.

He went back to the bedroom, to a small desk he'd noticed before, sat on the chair and began to go through the drawers and piece together the man's life.

He took care weaving through the files and paperwork he found in a side drawer, being sure to put things back where he'd found them. By the time he finished the task, he had a good idea of the man. He got a feel of Greenfield's childhood from a stack of old photos, one taken under giant Oak and Ash trees in some Midwestern town.

He had kept his military papers there, too, including three service bars and a silver star. Iraq patch. He'd also tucked away the overseas cards and letters from his wife, signed Rose, at the bottom of each missive. In that file, also letters written by Greenfield to Rose - but never sent - from Fallujah, the besieged Iraqi city. It sparked some hazy nightmarish memories in Hal. Perhaps they'd served together? He reached across his body with his left arm to replace the papers and noticed the ache there in that shoulder, remembered the slam of the bullet when it knocked him sideways, but nothing more came through, no matter how hard Hal concentrated.

He looked through a series of medical bills for infertility treatments, dated much later. Court papers filed six months ago regarding what looked like a nasty divorce.

Pangs of guilt interspersed with the fascination of another's most private moments set his emotions on a roller-coaster. A sense of invasion, but also of empathy. As brothers in arms. Almost.

That finally accomplished, Hal went to the kitchen and the

door he'd seen Greenfield walk through. He expected it to be locked but it wasn't.

The steps down were enshrouded in darkness but he found a switch that lit the whole basement. He descended into a large square concrete space. A washer-dryer sat in one corner and other than a few cardboard boxes that contained outdoor recreational equipment and another with toys geared for a toddler, there wasn't much. He was about to go back up when he noticed a grayed plywood sheet he hadn't seen earlier because it eerily mated up with the concrete. It was a flimsy door, not locked.

Without thinking, he put his right hand on the butt of the gun in his pocket and inched the door open, standing to one side, not sure what he might find.

A dining table dominated the middle of the room with a thick white unlit candle sitting in the middle. Even in just the light from the outside room, he saw a raft of scattered papers strewn over the entire surface. He found a light switch and a single bare bulb threw dim light over the space.

He examined the papers on the dining table. Photos and newspaper clipping, each featuring some aspect of Portman's life, movie posters, galas she'd attended, posed pictures with other stars. Her head shot again. Nothing stood out other that the sheer obsession it bespoke of Greenfield.

In one corner, another small table - resembling a miniature roll-top desk, also with a large candle, its wick blackened from use. A collection of knives, twelve in all, sat upon a red velvet table covering. A used rag, a honing stone and a jar of silver polish sat to the side. Again, the glamor head shot of Portman had been perched on the top of a small set of drawers.

They were mostly empty but in one, he found and paged through a sheaf of six loose pages torn from a small spiral notebook that depicted in scrawling pencil stick figure images. In one, an obviously large-breasted woman with a man who is shown stabbing her with a knife. In another, a woman lying prone with multiple knifes sticking out of her, and a third drawing showing a woman whose round eyeless head had been drawn separated from the stick figure female body by a bloody ax in a man's hands.

In another drawer, he found a page of copy paper on which was drawn - again in child-like hand - an image that called to mind an old guess-the-word game he once played somewhere. Another stick figure, again with circles representing breasts. It was shown being hanged from an equally artless gallows. The mystery word had been completed at the same time the hanging had - each letter corresponded to a pencil stroke part of the gallows:

D A M N A T I O N

Hal shivered, then put everything back the way it was. Repositioned the door. After climbing the stairs and flipping the light switch off, he exited the way he'd come in, remembering to lock the door and put the key back where he'd found it.

As he walked back to the Toyota, the sun was high in the morning sky. He stretched his arms out, pulled his knees up on by one. There was no pain, no shortness of breath that he'd been warned to look for. He felt excited but at the same time, a sense of dreadful foreboding gnawed at his guts and walked along with him. Greenfield's intentions were clear.

The right thing to do would be to warn the woman. But he had his orders from Betterton. A better course of action would be to simply go back out to the Edge warehouse and arrest Greenfield. Or leave and come back later and apprehend him. Maybe just inform Betterton and let the mystery room cops take him down.

Still, he had no idea how long Greenfield worked or when

he got off. Or if Greenfield would maybe feign illness and leave work early, go after the woman then. Or perhaps Greenfield was only fantasizing, playing basement games for his own gratification.

Or maybe he was planning to carry out some sort of murderous action soon, but just not today? He certainly had no confidence in his ability to pull off the FBI act and actually take Greenfield into custody.

But maybe he could make something else up. Maybe Greenfield could be accused of being a suspect in some terror plot aimed at his plant. Or maybe his intimate knowledge of the plant's security systems would help the FBI strengthen security against a foreign plot the FBI had knowledge of?

It confused Hal. He pulled over and went through the options again and again, the air conditioning blowing in his face, until he decided what to do.

***

After leaving Greenfield's house, Hal drove an hour north into the hills on the 2, cut across east on a two track and drove by the address Betterton had provided, scoping the place out. Portman lived in a ranch-style house on a slight rise surrounded by a three-foot adobe wall. It sat away from the road and, like many homes in southern California, a swimming pool had been built in back. A well-tended and obviously irrigated vegetable garden and a citrus orchard grew beyond the pool in back.

He drove past again and pulled into a field access a quarter mile away in a low area where the Toyota wouldn't be spotted, parked and then made his way under the mid-day sun across the neighbor's horse paddock, going from tree to tree for cover.

The house had three doors —the front, a back door and a side door exiting to a carport under which a black Cadillac SUV sat.

A lawn of lush grass surrounded the structure, also irrigated. Outside the wall, some shrubbery gave him good cover and he watched for signs of activity. A faint tinkle of music drifted over the hot air from somewhere.

He crept forward and stopped behind a bush at the corner of the carport. All the determination he'd felt before dried up. He realized he had no plan. What was he supposed to do? He couldn't just walk up, knock on the door and tell the woman someone was hunting her, that someone meant her serious harm, could he? And why also did he think the woman lived alone? He felt ridiculous. Exposed.

He was about to turn back when a woman he hadn't seen before rose from the pool and stood on the concrete apron, wringing her long blonde hair. Portman. She wore a barely-there black bikini, stepped around the ladder, went to a chaise lounge and began to towel off.

Her back was toward him. Hal considered using the opportunity to back away and forget the whole bad idea but noticed a large flowering bougainvillea next to the house. He stepped quickly over the grass and stood behind it. He noticed a slanted door, likely some root cellar for storing the produce Portman was growing.

Hal looked back the way he came. What was he doing? What did he think he would accomplish? But now he was stuck there, too close to make any move to leave without risking being seen. He was glued to the spot, watching the woman.

She lifted a towel and passed it over her skin so frustratingly slow, he had an urge to ... to run up ... to help her ... dry off more quickly. She worked her way around her shoulders, then her upper back. She was all curves. Even at that distance, Hal could see the creamy texture of her skin, imagined the feel of it. She toweled her lower back, still facing away and just when Hal wanted to help her get to that one spot on her back she couldn't reach, she bent forward and began smoothing the terrycloth across her long legs.

He should get the hell out of there, he knew, but he remained hidden. He felt passion rise through his flesh, an urge to touch her, a sudden illogical need to possess this woman. Soft jazz came from a blue tooth speaker on a glass table. The hot breeze rustled the leaves. He had a fleeting thought that maybe the woman knew he was there, watching. But that couldn't be the case, could it?

Her fingers slid under the straps of her bikini top and with slow and measured moves slipped it off. She stood in the sunlight still facing away from him. She laid the garment over the table and then picked up a bottle of something, squeezed out a creamy liquid into her hand and began smoothing it over her neck and her shoulders and her chest. She slid her swimsuit bottom down and as if a dancer with perfect control, slowly smoothed the lotion over her first one foot and then the other, over one leg and then the other, over the curves of back and the rounds of her hips. Hal was beside himself. Every impulse in his body wanted to run to her. To have her. The ache he felt became more intense, almost as if pain were a woman that hugged him close across his whole body.

She moved. She spread a towel and laid down on her stomach. Each action seemed to play out in slow motion in Hal's mind. She had the most amazing beautiful tanned skin. No tan-lines. Jesus, Hal thought. She must sunbath in the nude all the time.

He stayed perfectly still. Her face was turned toward him, eyes closed. Now the urge to get the hell out of there seized him. What he was doing was way wrong. He was despicable, no better than Greenfield. He tried to not breathe but then realized he was breathing too fast, not right.

Still, she had the most amazing ass. The woman stirred and

turned her head away from Hal and came to a repose again. A Madonna in a dreamy renaissance painting. A Venus on a half shell. A Bathsheba, to be adored and lusted after.

That thought got Hal going. He slipped away, moving from bush to hiding place, shrub to cover, feeling pain in all his joints. He finally found his way back to the car, all the while berating himself for his utter failure at the job he was given, the task he'd been trusted with. A failed human being.

He was having trouble now. His vision was off. The road back was not quite in focus. A headache had built. Even his jaw hurt. He'd been out too long. He was taking big breaths, as if the air was devoid of oxygen. He relished in the misery.

He deserved everything he got.

***

"Good on you for the Greenfield info. We thought we were protecting him from evil. But what the hell did you think you were going to accomplish over at the women's place?"

Hal felt the heat of his memories rise into his face, the shame. "I… protecting her from Greenfield… warn her. I don't know what I was thinking. I'm sorry. I screwed up."

"Don't say those words here," Betterton said. "We're all sorry sad sacks here." He studied Hal. "Hey, Are you okay, man? You were out there a long time."

Hal had almost recovered. He hurt like he'd run a marathon yesterday but his breathing was normal now. He waved the question away.

"What's going to happen now?" Hal asked.

"What's going to happen is once you're back strong enough, you're going back out there and sticking with Greenfield like flies on flypaper. Somehow get him to abort this dead-end thing he's got for Portman."

"Coat of Invisibility?"

"I told you, no can do. So you'll have to be on your toes."

***

Greenfield didn't waste any time. Somehow, despite Portman's rejection the night before, he managed to convince her to hook up. Hal followed them out on the 2 into the hill country north of the suburbs, tailing way behind. Traffic was light but in the dark, headlights were anonymous.

He pulled off the two-track in the low spot he's used last time and walked without worry through the paddock. At the house, a Caddy and a Corvette sat in the gravel drive. Lights were on.

He didn't bother trying to be secretive but walked right up to the house and peered through what appeared to be a bedroom window, lit from within. They were already sitting on the bed, laughing, pawing at each other, she with a glass of red wine, he with white powder like errant makeup on his nose.

He walked to the front but the door was locked. As was the side and the back door. He would have t break in. Somehow put a stop to whatever was going to happen.

He didn't think this an innocent encounter. He'd discovered too many things about these people. One of them was going to end up dead, or worse. He'd have to wait until something happened to make his move. He fingered the FBI badge in his pocket, felt the heft of the Glock against his right thigh.

Then, he remembered the bush he'd hid behind watching the woman. Remembered the twin wooden doors set at a low slant. A root cellar, or old bomb shelter. Either way, it might give him a way in. He could be ready then, when it came down, not standing outside deciding which window to break through.

The double doors had a Yale lock across the hasp. He looked

around and found a small garden spade and easily pried the hasp from the rotting wood. Easing one of the doors open, a set of stairs led down. He was immediately hit with a wave of intense cold, a smell. Dirt? Worms? Decay? A whirring sound.

At the bottom of the stairs he pulled out his key chain and flicked on a high-powered tiny flashlight and pointed it at the source of the noise, upper left. A small AC unit was blasting full on. Wires extended down from it and he saw a contraption he'd only seen in bars and wineries: A cool bot. He could see his breath. But why?

He turned into the room. He saw what looked like a bouncy-bouncy, that kids' carnival activity. Mounds of inflated vinyl on the floor near the side wall. The room seemed empty otherwise. It confused him. From above, he heard a wail. Passion? Pain?

He hurried along but before he took two steps, he tripped over one of the balloons and almost fell. When he caught himself, he shined his light on the structure.

Shiny plastic reflections. Bare feet, wrapped in a clear plastic like bubble wrap. And next to that, more wrapped feet. He pointed the light up and around and saw the naked bodies, all of them. Wrapped and sealed. Jesus, he whispered. Jesus.

He hesitated but then lit up the face of the body on the end of the row. It looked - he couldn't be sure, because the face was disfigured - the eyes had been clawed out somehow, the man's face swollen and disfigured. But the face had a large brown birthmark at the left hairline.

He stepped back, almost dropped his light. It was Williamson. His Bridge partner. How…?

It came to him then. Clicked in place. The rules. One of them anyway. This was the real room. Just as the backyard swimming pool was real.

Games had been played here. Men, he now surmised, had

paid the price of lust, had lost the battle with evil. The men in this room. The men in his room. The Bridge room.

He went down the row, knowing what he'd find. Armon was there, naked, his face so mangled he was hardly recognizable. At his waist held in place with tightly wrapped plastic, were his bloody fingers and his teeth and his genitals. And there was DeShawn, same. And the others. He came to the last body, at the end. The corpse had been badly disfigured. The eyes were bloody holes. All the fingers had been cut away, as had the genitals. He couldn't recognize the face, but he recognized the body. The body he'd seen so many times in the mirror, the body that had conveyed him to foreign wars.

He cast the light up, toward the left shoulder and saw what he knew he would. The healed bullet hole.

He turned and threw up on the dirt floor.

A wail again from upstairs. He spit and wiped his mouth, turned and found the stairs up. He was done down there. Another wail as he gained the first floor.

A lamp was lit in the living room and faint light came through an open door down the hall. He crept along the wall and came to the open door, chanced a quick look inside.

The women had the man on the bed and she held a rope tied around his neck, taut. She strained at it. The knot under Greenfield's chin tightened and Greenfield choked, turned a dusky color and fell slack.

Hal pulled back, waited, looked again. The woman had her back toward him and he remembered seeing that back before, naked then. He gathered in the surroundings. Greenfield was laying flat on the bed, his bloody left wrist caught in some sort of contraption that looked for all the world like a small animal trap. His breath came sporadic and sonorous. The woman was fiddling with something. A shotgun stood against the far wall. He noticed a selection of sex toys on the bedside stand and a

5 inch serrated knife on the top of a TV tray. Hal ducked back, trying to think of what to do. He had to do something.

He snuck a look again. In that flash, the woman was holding a Black and Decker drill and testing it out. Greenfield was coming to, his free arm moving, his head writhing back and forth on the bed.

He thought about pulling the gun but he was afraid he'd shoot someone. Forget the gun, forget the badge. He knew combat, knew hand-to-hand. He didn't know cop stuff. So, a bull rush.

He came around the corner and ran toward her, crashed his shoulder into her and knocked he off her feet. But she came back up almost immediately with a baseball bat in her hands. Hal thought incongruously how he hadn't seen that coming. It hit him on the shoulder as he ducked. Pain seared through his right side, vision becoming blue-black but after staggering, he came back at her again.

She was at the wall and grabbing the shotgun, was swinging it up toward him. Hal crashed into her with his full weight, driving her back. At the same time, he grabbed the barrel of the gun and shoved the wood stock hard into her mid-section. The gun went off, the noise so loud, Hal was deafened.

He pulled the gun from Portman, turned it around and shot her in the face.

***

Greenfield had come to.

I'm leaving now," Hal told him. "There's ten dead men in the basement. There's this shit storm up here. I'm calling 911 now from your phone. I'm surprised she didn't take it from you."

He lifted the shotgun, aimed it away at the walls and fired

off all the rounds left until the gun clicked. The booms hurt his ears. Neighbors would hear but he didn't care.

"Who are you, man?" Greenfield wailed. Blood came from his mouth from where he'd apparently lost a tooth. "What…?" Hal had not undone Greenfield's left wrist from the trap.

"Let's just say I'm your guardian angel. Makeup any story you want. Tell the cops whatever makes sense to you. Tell them about me, I don't care. They won't believe you and they can't prove I was ever here. But if the story is good enough, you'll do okay.

Hal put the gun in Greenfield's right arm, making sure Greenfield gasped it, and left the house quickly. Sirens were audible. He didn't need to call 911.

***

"I don't know whether to congratulate you or send you directly to hell, Michaels," Betterton said. "You don't take orders very well and you got more than a few quirks of your own."

Hal looked down. Guilty.

"But don't we all? You saved the room. So there's that."

The red phone rang. Betterton shot Hal a look. They'd been waiting on the boss. Betterton picked it up and mostly listened. Hal fidgeted in the metal chair. He couldn't wait to tell the guys.

But Hal did wait. Eventually, after nods and yes, ma'ams, Betterton hung up.

"All good Michaels, he said. "Greenfield will probably get off. Self-defense. But he may end up doing some time for stalking with intent. Hopefully, he learns a thing or two."

"The woman, she was…evil.

"She was the devil, Michaels. But the boss says you guys are all moving downtown. All of the room."

Hal wanted to ask what that meant but decided against it.

"It's a huge deal," Betterton said. "For all you guys. You came through, man."

Hal sat back, feeling at peace for the first time in a long time.

"Me, all I get is an empty room again, waiting to be filled. Maybe Gin Rummy this go-around. I'm tired of Bridge. Seems like we've played it forever."

About the Authors

Stephen L. Brayton

Stephen L. Brayton is a Sixth Degree Black Belt in the American Taekwondo Association and a Marketing Associate for a software company. Current publications include Alpha, the first of his Mallory Petersen action mystery series, and Night Shadows, the first in a supernatural series featuring a Homicide detective and an FBI agent.

He is the editor and contributing author of *The Peace Tree Mystery*, a story set in the Knoxville, Iowa/Lake Red Rock area. He has also been published in numerous anthologies of fiction, poems in Lyrical Iowa 2018-2024, and articles in the Nov/Dec '22 & '23 issues of Plant Engineering.

Kendall Klym

In addition to winning the Tartt First Fiction Award for Step Lightly: Stories, Dr. Kendall Klym has won numerous awards and has been published in literary journals including *Puerto del Sol*, *Hunger Mountain*, and *Fiction International*. Klym is a three-time honorable mention winner of the Great American Fiction Contest and has won writing fellowships at the Fairhope Center for the Writing Arts, the Martha's Vineyard Institute of Creative Writing, and Monson Arts. Two of his stories were nominated for a Pushcart Prize. Klym holds a PhD in English with a concentration in Fiction Writing from the University of Wales, Aberystwyth.

Deb Miller

Deb Miller enjoys writing unique short stories that showcase unusual professions, settings, or historical periods. Her contributions to print anthologies include "The Haunting of Four Mile Creek," 2023. And "Mustn't Tell" 2024 published in a suspense anthology. Her interests include traveling the world by cruise ship, binge-watching ancient archeology videos, and a previous career in IT. Deb is working on her debut novel titled "Fox Hunt on the Prairie."

Joann Schissel

Joann Schissel is author of *Before It's Too Late*, a novel released in 2024 about mother-daughter estrangement. She has several short stories published and earned an Honorable Mention in the University of Iowa's Write Now Micro Story Contest in 2024. Her fiction writing interest began after retiring from decades of employment in marketing and graphic design in Des Moines, IA. She currently lives on a vineyard with her husband and together they own and operate a winery and write novels.

Michael Van Natta

Michael Van Natta has been hard at writing fiction for the last thirty years and has published a novel, *Leo's Birds*, and many short stories. He is the founder and long-time facilitator of the Marion County Writer's Workshop (est. 2003), and co-owner of *Back Roads Literary Review* (est. 2022). He and his wife, Joann, also own and operate Nearwood Winery and Vineyards in Knoxville, Iowa. He is a retired family physician who loves to play golf, guitar and fish for trout.

ACKNOWLEDGMENTS

This volume of the Back Rounds Literary Review, as well as all the previous volumes, has been brought into existence largely due to writers who do what writers of fiction do – be persistent, have at it, then get better. I'd like to thank members of the Marion County Writers Workshop who have engaged in the art and science of writing over the years, those who have sat at desks and keyboards for years, laboring over the love of story, of the written word on the page, those who have come and gone from the group, and those who were there at the beginning twenty-one years ago.

Writing is difficult, as M. Scott Peck said about life. But once that is known, writing becomes less difficult. Every newbie writer has dreams of becoming famous, or at least known for writing. Very few get there. Some get to somewhere along the way and give up. Others find that somewhere to be sufficient. And others yet find the road itself – the improvement, the gratification of writing and having written, of the compunction to write – to be sufficient.

The Anthology was created as another waypoint on that road, a vehicle by which to travel it, and a fuel to help propel the writer toward a destination unknown, or wished for, or purely fictional. But maybe more than anything, it has been a provisioning method for the journey yet ahead.

In its mission, this publication works to support new and emerging writers on this journey toward an imagined destination. It is not the first our authors have written and it will not be the last, those who know that along the road where the action is, the destination beyond control.

I especially want to thank Stephen Brayton, Mary Walker, Larry Brown, and Teresa Tallman who, along with my lovely and patient wife, Joann Schissel, were there at the formative stages of this effort and who have in large measure been supportive in seeking to fulfill our mission.

There are many others I could include on this list: Susan Taylor Chehak, a mentor at the University of Iowa Summer Writers Festival, chief among them. And the many writers there and elsewhere I've met along the road I've traveled.

Visit www.BackroadsLiteraryReview.com
for more information about us or to purchase our
other publications.